TO SCATTER STONES

m.t. dohaney

RAGWEED
THE ISLAND PUBLISHER

COPYRIGHT © M.T. Dohaney, 1992

ISBN 0-921556-23-3

With thanks to the Canada Council for its kind support.

Cover Drawing, "The Shell Gatherers"
by Janice Udell, courtesy of the Christina Parker Gallery,
St. John's, Newfoundland

Edited by Lynn Henry

Cover and book design by Catherine Matthews

Printed and bound in Canada by
Imprimerie d'Éditions Marquis Ltée

for
RAGWEED PRESS
P.O. Box 2023
Charlottetown, Prince Edward Island
Canada C1A 7N7

CANADIAN CATALOGUING IN PUBLICATION DATA

Dohaney, M. T.
    To scatter stones
    ISBN 0-921556-23-3
I. Title.

PS8557.0257T6 1992   C813'.54   C92-098535-1
PR9199.3.D64T6 1992

For Roge

To everything there is a season, and a
time for every purpose under heaven:
A time to be born and a time to die ...
A time to scatter stones
and a time to gather stones ...

Ecclesiastes 3:1-8

PART I

*A*lthough it is well into May, a winter storm pelted St. John's during the night. Big water-logged flakes of snow blew across the harbour and settled on the city's steep, narrow streets in uneven mounds of yellow slush. And as if this mess wasn't bad enough in itself, around daylight the temperature took a sudden dip and turned the slush into lumps of ice. It is the type of morning that makes people say, "You wouldn't turn a stray dog outdoors."

But I relish this mess of weather—although I'm probably the only one on the Island who does. Indeed, when my clock radio snapped on at seven this morning and I was treated to a detailed description of the storm that had moved in during the night from Labrador, I let out a gleeful whoop. The news of this unexpected hodge-podge of wind, sleet, snow and frost instantly warmed the cockles of my heart, as it would have anyone's in my line of business. It was exactly what I needed to pitch my sales quota over the top.

"Eat your hearts out, travel agents in Vancouver and Montreal," I gloated, as I hung on to every colourful storm adjective the announcer used. "Don't you wish your offices were down here where spring is only a date on a calendar?"

Because the dampness of the morning had already leaked in through the clapboards of my ground-floor apartment, my bedroom was as cold as a tomb, so I arched up on my elbow to rummage through the bedclothes for the thermostat on my electric blanket, and hiked it up a notch or two. As I leaned upwards, I caught sight of my face in the bureau mirror at the far end of the room and my scoundrelly smile reminded me of a scene from an old Danny Kaye movie. In the movie, Danny was a New York City cab driver and, like me, he had awakened to a city caught off-guard by a dastardly storm. As he peered out his bedroom window at the pedestrians hurrying up and down the sidewalks with their shoulders hunched to fend off the cold, a rascally grin spread over his face. The grin had widened as he converted each rain-soaked head, each mud-splattered pant leg, into potential cab fares.

After I jacked up the thermostat, I squirrelled back into the flannel bedsheets, although by this time they felt as clammy as if they had been left on the garden clothesline until well after the fog had rolled in. I lay there savouring the sound of the storm as it battered itself against my street-facing window, my gaze riveted on my white, lacy curtains as they quivered against the casings, bracing themselves for the next onslaught of wind.

I congratulated myself on having had the good sense to rent an apartment near the city centre, and close enough to the Sperry Travel Agency to walk to work. Now, the announcer's warning about unploughed roads only heightened my pleasure in the storm. I would be able to get to the office, and I'd be on hand to take the telephone calls, which I was certain would come incessantly. All of the callers would be wanting me to get them off the Island immediately, and to some place where the sun could be counted on to shine. And they would all talk to me in the same injured tone, as though some mischievous god had placed them in a climate for which their sensibilities were ill-suited.

Of course, I knew I wouldn't be able to do anything for them for at least several days and, of course, I knew they knew this as well. It is difficult enough getting airline seating off the Island at this time of year without the added complication of shut-down runways; and according to the news report, the runways would be out of operation for at least twenty-four hours. Even if extra flights were put on, I was certain there would still be a long waiting list after the runways were cleared.

But I was sure my clients wouldn't be bothered by a short delay. Just making arrangements for some future getaway would be enough to pacify even the most disgruntled amongst them. And by the time they got around to leaving the Island, none of them would care a whit whether the fury of the northeast wind had petered out, or whether the fishing vessels were cowering inside the Narrows.

The day I signed the lease on my downtown apartment, I knew I was sacrificing sunlit rooms for proximity to work, and now, almost twelve months later, I am certain that proximity to work is its only virtue. I live on the lower level of an old house, on a street so steep I drive up and down it with one foot on the gas pedal and the other hovering over the brake. All of the houses are built cheek by jowl, so there isn't enough room between them to swing a cat, so to speak—let alone room enough for the sun to angle in through the small, ground-floor windows.

Often when I'm on my way home from work, worn from the day, I'll stop at the bottom of the street and look up with dismay at the hill I still have to climb, and at the row of flat-topped houses edging up against the uneven sidewalk. The houses need paint and the street needs paving. Indeed, the whole area has such a scuffed look, I wonder why I don't move to a more inviting section of the city. And sometimes, when whimsy gets the better of me, I wonder what would happen if the house at the very top of the street were to fall over. I imagine all of the other houses on the street tumbling down, knocking into each other, like the houses of cards I used to build when I was a child only to see Grandmother unintentionally topple them by forgetting to ease the kitchen door open or shut.

After the radio announcer had prodded me several times to get up, saying it was ten-past and then half-past the hour, I reluctantly stopped revelling in the storm outside my window. I flung back the bedclothes and gingerly stepped out on the small rose-coloured area rug covering the linoleum floor. I had bought the rug in Montreal, paying almost a month's salary for it, a price that had prompted my husband—now my ex-husband—to accuse me of wanton spending. Leonard had a tendency to magnify his nouns with extravagant adjectives—although, at the time of the purchase, even I had felt that the price of the rug was bordering on the obscene.

Once up, I immediately went to the window and searched for a peephole in the snow-covered panes. When I saw the mess outside, I was instantly convinced it was the type of day to wear something outlandish and exotic—something warm, office-appropriate, but with a hint of the South Seas.

I rushed to the bathroom, and all the while I was in the shower I mentally searched my closet for the proper outfit—the proper colour to set a proper mood. But I found nothing suitable, so I told myself I would resume my search for real and in earnest as soon as I got back to the bedroom.

I have a theory about colour—a theory that probably caused the demise of my marriage to Leonard almost as much as the reappearance of Monica Wheeler did. Then, like now, I was convinced that there is a positive correlation between the colour of the clothes I wear to the office and the quality and the quantity of the

. 10 .

travel bookings I make. My theory is loosely tied to the power of suggestion. I believe, for example, that if I wear clothes to the office that are reminiscent of more benign climates, my clients will be more apt to buy travel packages to faraway places, rather than settling for a short hop to Montreal or even to Florida.

Indeed, I'm so convinced that this correlation exists, that in summer when it is so hot in St. John's you can smell new asphalt being put down as far away as Long's Hill, I always wear seafoam-green dresses, and skirts and blouses the colour of the sails on those sporty little boats you see tacking into the wind on the Mediterranean.

To Leonard's chagrin, and often acute embarrassment, I was very vocal about my theory during our short period of cleaving only unto each other. That I had no body of research to support this theory never daunted me from stating it as though it had been founded upon years and years of well-documented studies. And Leonard's cringing in the presence of his colleagues over his wife's unscholarly pronouncements never for one moment curbed me from making them.

In all fairness to myself, it is a fact that my branch of the Sperry Travel Agency now has the highest sales record per capita of all the Sperry branches across Canada. And my speedy rise to Assistant Manager in the Montreal office was directly related to the number of sales I brought in. Therefore, if I see a positive connection between my colour-coded office clothes and my high sales record, who can blame me?

When I returned to my bedroom after showering, I began a frenzied rummaging in my closet for that "just right" outfit to wear to the office. I hurriedly pushed aside hanger after hanger, vowing that my next apartment wouldn't have closets so small that the racks resembled a clearance sale at Eaton's. After several minutes of this rummaging, my search resulted in a pile of rejected clothes humped on my bed, and a long-sleeved blouse and matching full skirt in my hand. I was convinced that the skirt's multi-coloured print was exactly what I needed to make my clients choose Spain over Florida, and Africa over Arizona.

I then brought both pieces of clothing to the window to search for wrinkles. Although I found plenty, on account of the cramped closets, I quickly dismissed any notion of getting out the ironing board. Instead, I hurriedly tossed the skirt over my head and wriggled it down to my waist and then hauled on the blouse and quickly tucked it inside the skirt. While still in the process of zippering and buttoning, I raced to the kitchen to start breakfast. Even in my rush, though, I did not fail to notice the garish wallpaper as I hurried past the bathroom and spare bedroom, and I reaffirmed my intent to badger my landlord into re-papering my apartment in a pattern that wouldn't resemble the gnarly, sun-shy weeds that grow between the houses.

Because my galley-shaped kitchen has only one small window, I have to turn on a light even in daytime, and as I reached across the sink for the electrical switch, my head bumped into a potted plant that hangs, in a gallows-like pot, from my ceiling. It is a plant Leonard gave me. A birthday present. It is an azalea, and Leonard, being a stickler for detail and refined definitions—a trait that makes him an excellent taxation lawyer—had explained that it was of the *Heath* family, a hybrid of the genus *Rhododendron*. He had stated with certitude that in no time at all it would be in full bloom. Full *pink* bloom.

But many months, one divorce and a move to St. John's have come and gone since that statement and there isn't even a trace of a bloom. Actually, there's barely a trace of life—the plant is now only a sun-starved, long-stalked shadow of its original virile self.

In the several months that I've been in the apartment, I've moved this azalea to different locations—probably more to prove Leonard wrong (when the blooms do come they won't be pink) than to preserve its life—but the moves have done little to prevent its lingering demise. After I had unintentionally jostled it this morning, I reached up to stop it from bobbing about in its macrame holder, and sternly told myself that my reason for keeping it alive is not worthy of me. I vowed that one of these days I'd toss it out on its ear and cavalierly say it was not fated to survive, just as Leonard had tossed out our marriage with the same limp explanation.

The day Leonard was scouting our Montreal condominium for a suitable southern-exposured window for the azalea, he had remarked in a pretend off-handed way that I couldn't kill this breed of plant no matter how much I neglected it. I had let the remark slide by, unchallenged. Of late, Leonard had been hinting that I was neglecting the marriage, although I could never get him to pinpoint the exact area of neglect. In hindsight, I realize he was searching for evidence of neglect; he needed it to justify his ongoing adultery and his upcoming leave-taking.

He was, however, arrow sharp in his criticism of my treatment of the flora he was constantly bringing home and abandoning to my care. Over the months of our marriage I had allowed several pots of geraniums, purple violets, baby fern and various other bits and pieces of foliage to choke to death from unslaked thirst. I guess he reasoned that if I could neglect the plants he hauled home, I could just as easily neglect a marriage he had co-founded.

Actually, I still allow plants to parch themselves into oblivion. Only a week ago I tossed out the withered remains of a St. Patrick's Day shamrock, its roots caked in soil so hard it could be used for a city sidewalk.

Sometimes I wonder what character flaw of mine prompts people to give me plants—gifts that set me up to become a serial killer. Why, for instance, am I given creeping ivy instead of champagne, and rubber plants instead of chocolate truffles? And why am I made to feel like a psychopath when the dried-out remains of a yellow chrysanthemum follow a pinched and peaked, pale to the point of death, poinsettia into the garbage can.

Once, when I told a girlfriend how disappointed I was that Leonard had given me a plant for my birthday when I would have preferred some carnal lingerie, she gave a whoop of laughter at my preposterous expectations and proceeded to make an analogy between my personality and Leonard's. She said that if we were ships, Leonard would be the Queen Elizabeth—a sure-as-fire money-making operation—and I would be an antiquated exploration vessel belonging to some ancient explorer, ploughing the seas, my bow filled with fanciful notions of unlimited possibilities. Her assessment wasn't totally apt, but close enough not to warrant denial.

I'm not certain why I married Leonard, or for that matter, why he married me. I think it had to do with timing. We needed the union—needed it desperately—and in our rush for matrimony we failed to focus on needs that neither of us could fulfill for the other. When I am striving for honesty, I have to admit that even without my colour theory and even without the reappearance of Leonard's para-legal, our union would still have died—much like my plants, which always end up falling over under their own weight.

Leonard, an expert in corporate taxation, and no slouch either in the ways and means of dissolving a marriage—his, mine, ours—had his beginnings in Toronto. It was a rooting in asphalt and concrete, a rooting that connotes sophistication and rational thinking. He believed then (and probably still does) that the physical environment surrounding our formative years is largely responsible for making us who we are and what we become. He told me he learned this in one of the sociology courses he took in his undergraduate years before he headed into law. There have been times when I have wondered whether he would have been so quick to accept this "environment-is-all" theory if, like me, his beginnings had been in the Cove, and if, like me, one of his earliest memories was of being hit in the face with a salty whitecap that the northeast wind had booted over the beach.

However, even if there's only a grain of truth to Leonard's theory, it certainly would explain our widely different perspectives on life. Leonard is a realist, and I should have recognized that we had diametrically opposed personalities when his mother told me that Leonard always returned his library books on time. My library books were frequently stamped "overdue" in big, admonishing red letters.

I was, and still am, a romantic. As a melancholy young girl I frequently wallowed in dreams of shipwrecks where all hands on board made it safely to shore. The shore was always the kelpy landwash behind our house, and in particular, that spit of rocky beach I could see from my bedroom window. I imagined that the suitcases the survivors lugged up the beach were chock-full of laces as fine as spider webs, and packed with silks and satins in colours as varied as the pansies Grandmother planted each summer in the front garden, and which she never quite successfully kept out of the reach of the sheep.

Shortly after we met, I confided some of my childhood fantasies to Leonard, giving special attention to the one about an old mansion I had been convinced I was going to inherit. The donor was some obscure relative and the house had been unoccupied for several years. (I wanted neither the pain of loss, nor the guilt of eviction to spoil my inheritance.) I told Leonard of how I revelled in the notion of searching the nooks and crannies of this once-genteel home and coming upon brown photographs, antiquated lavender-smelling dresses, passionate love letters and other odds and ends of past lives.

Leonard, who had been getting his law practice in corporate taxation underway, said that just to heat a drafty old relic like the one I was describing would suck the last cent out of my bank account. As well, its upkeep would be so outrageously expensive no one would want to buy it. This conversation took place in Leonard's Montreal apartment and as he talked he nodded in the direction of Toronto, which I presumed from his gestures was through the back wall of his livingroom.

As he talked, he bobbed his head towards the beige wall over his sofa and in a tone that gave no room for opinions to the contrary stated, "You wouldn't even be able to unload it *up there*." From the arch of his eyebrows I gathered that if I couldn't unload it *up there*, where the current rage was buying "fixer-uppers," then where could I unload it? He called my fanciful bequest "a realtor's nightmare." He said the words in a dismissing tone, annoyed with himself for talking such tomfoolishness when his time could be better spent arranging his briefcase into compartments, so that one aspect of his work day didn't mingle with the other.

Although Leonard never said so, I knew that if he had been the one indulging in such make-believe, he would have come upon raw cash in that mansion rather than finding useless memorabilia. He'd want raw cash, not just because it would be easier to keep out of the sight of the Revenue Department, but because it would eliminate all that digging about in dusty old trunks. Searching nooks and crannies for remnants of unrequited love and tag ends of yesterday's lives held not the slightest appeal for him. Scouring taxation documents to shake down loopholes in federal and provincial tax laws was more to his liking.

Actually, the more I think about it, the more easily I can be persuaded that physical surroundings may indeed have a bearing on one's personality. I, for instance, would probably be other than I am, had my first breath been gulped in some bustling metropolitan hospital in the heart of Toronto or Vancouver, rather than in a house that huddled into a cliff and stared fearfully into the Atlantic Ocean. And I probably wouldn't have this gnawing longing to be remembered if, in budding womanhood, I had been able to gouge "Tessie loves Dennis" into cement sidewalks, instead of scratching it in wet sand where it instantly disappeared with the incoming tide. And I'd probably also be willing to settle for cremation when my time comes and be reconciled to having my ashes scattered hither and yon, instead of coveting a spot on Dickson's Hill beside the other Corrigans, whose slabs of granite are already leaning into the wind.

My need to be remembered has been a constant in my life and I still manage to work it into many fanciful dreams—the most preferred one taking place about fifty years after my demise. A group will be sitting around a livingroom engrossed in lively conversation and someone will say, "Well, it's like Tess Corrigan always said ..." The speaker will then quote some witticism of mine so right for the occasion that others will follow suit, detailing anecdote after anecdote—not mine, but attributed to me anyway because anything less would exclude them from the inner circle.

When I was a very young girl, fourteen or so, I longed to be remembered as a doomed heroine. I wanted to be struck down with a fatal disease, although certainly not one that would shrivel the flesh and make my body an ugly corpse. Tuberculosis was my disease of choice. I would be wan and waxen, dead in the bloom of life. There I'd lie, hauntingly beautiful, my black, fresh-ly-washed hair fanned out against the pure white lining of my made-in-the-Cove casket—a memory burnt forever into the eyes of those who gazed upon my still form.

Now, if on top of what I've meted out to you so far, I tell you that at the height of the Great Depression, a relative of mine spit his chew of tobacco into the Sunday collection because the basket had been held too long under his poverty-stricken nose, you'll probably leap to the conclusion—a conclusion I eventually drew—that Leonard and I should never have been joined in holy matrimony. And you'll probably think that it is a marvel the marriage lasted as long as it did (two years, plus a Sunday) before it was "rended asunder." But do not leap to the conclusion that the rending was painless, or that we became un-joined without suffering scorch or scathe.

This morning after I had steadied the ailing azalea plant, I continued to linger in my kitchen, woolgathering, as Grandmother would say, and not making any attempt to prepare my breakfast. Finally, after a guilty look at the clock over the stove, I hurriedly began to prepare the meal, going from fridge to stove to cupboard, locating and carrying—milk, bread, coffee mug. I grabbed a fork from the cutlery drawer to jab at the toaster, which refuses to give up the toast of its own accord. I began to fish out the burning bread, but not soon enough—it was already burnt black. I then took both slices to the sink and attempted to scrape their surfaces to a more accept-able brown, and within a few seconds black scrapings covered the bottom of the steel sink. It looked for all the world as though thousands of ants had come up out of the drain and were too mesmerized to move one way or the other.

But even as my hands were engaged in getting the meal ready, my mind stayed on the malingering azalea, recalling a day on the Trans-Canada Highway, near the cross-over between New Brunswick and Nova Scotia, when I had come within a hair's breadth of dumping the plant by the side of the road.

I was on my way to Newfoundland, hoping that a move back home and a new job would be exactly what I needed to put the last couple of years behind me. Sperry Travel had decided to open a branch office in St. John's and I was offered the opportunity to manage it. I was still raw and bleeding from my divorce and I had wanted to be as far away from Leonard as possible. In desperation, like a drowning man grabbing at a floating log, I had headed for home, the back seat of my car piled high with the spoils of my past life, the azalea plant propped securely between a box of books and my winter clothes. Just before coming into Amherst, a car in front of me had suddenly switched lanes, forcing me to lurch to a stop. The plant had tumbled to the floor, and in the process dumped a full pot of soil into the bag of sandwiches I had packed for my lunch. I had immediately pulled to the side of the road and tossed out the gravel-filled sandwiches, and I had been severely tempted to follow suit with the azalea plant.

My telephone rang in the middle of this wool-gathering, just as I was settling down to eat my breakfast. It was my secretary, informing me that she wouldn't be able to get to the office on account of the storm. After I hung up the receiver I chastised myself for allowing an azalea plant to send me rummaging in the past, especially on a morning that held such promise for business. Despite the scolding, though, I continued to remember—even going back so far, for no accountable reason, to a conversation I had overheard when I was about eleven years old.

I had been sitting at Grandmother's dining room table crayoning in a colouring book Mother had sent me from the States. Mabel Furlong, or Butcher Fred's Mabel, as she was called in the Cove, had dropped in for a visit with Grandmother and, as usual at such times, I was banished to another room because "little pitchers have big ears."

But I always managed to overhear the conversations anyway, and on this particular day, while my fingers deftly moved a yellow crayon within the outlines of a paper clown, my ears were cocked in the direction of the voices in the kitchen. The conversation was only a remnant of the same one that had gone on for several weeks.

Mabel's stepdaughter, Bridie, was getting married and Mabel was dead set against the match. Over a cup of tea and in a severe voice—the voice she must have used on Bridie that morning—Mabel related the latest confrontation.

"So Bertha girl," she had said, picking up the tag end of yesterday's talk, "I had it out with her this morning." Mabel clinked her cup down in her saucer and I knew she would be holding her hands, latticework fashion, over the mouth of the cup, the way she always did when the conversation was more important than the tea. And I knew Mabel's mouth would be pulled taut, giving her face a right-minded look that showed her exasperation with trying to talk sense into Bridie—or for that matter, into any of the Furlong tribe.

Mabel had continued to speak in her no-nonsense tone. "So I up and said to her not mincing me words, 'Yer in love with marriage, me girl. Not with Andrew Power.' " She then offered an aside that was aimed at bringing Grandmother over to her way of thinking. "Ye knows yerself, Bertha girl, he'll never amount to more than a pinch of henshit. And God bless the mark, but he has a face on him like the stern of a dory." Mabel's voice dropped resignedly, "So tell me, girl, what does she see in him?"

Grandmother never liked to take sides in neighbourhood squabbles and I knew she would slide away from this one by saying, as she usually did in similar situations, that everyone is entitled to his fancy, like the old woman said when she kissed a cow. But this morning the platitude didn't sit well with Mabel.

"For the lovin' honour of God, Bertha girl, don't talk such nonsense," Mabel said crossly. "Who in the hell wants to kiss a cow?" Her voice shivered. "Not that I wouldn't rather that than kiss Andrew Power."

Mabel had gone on to say that she loved Bridie as much as if she had been her own flesh and blood and she didn't want her to get into a marriage like the one she, herself, had gotten into. She then detailed her own marriage to the widower Fred, and ended by saying she wouldn't have minded any of it—not the long hours in the butcher shop stuffing tubs of sausage meat into fathoms of sheep gut, not even thanklessly bringing up Fred's saucy-faced, half-grown boys, if only the marriage bed had been satisfying; if only for one moment— her voice underscored the one—if only for *one* moment, her toes had curled with wanting.

Grandmother must have thought the conversation was turning scandalous because I heard her embarrassed cough. Within a few seconds her chair scraped the floor as she stretched to look into the dining room to see if I was listening. To assure her I had been concentrating on my colouring book and hadn't heard a word that had been said, I clutched the yellow crayon so hard it cracked right across the centre and afterwards hung in its paper wrapper like a broken-winged duck.

It was years before I fully understood the meaning of those words Mabel spoke, but the sadness in her voice etched itself into my soul right then and there and stayed with me ever after. In fact, in my highly-charged adolescence, Mabel became a tragic figure. She was a woman tied to a man who knew all about cuts of meat and links of sausage, but nothing, absolutely nothing, about the mysteries of the marriage bed.

And the tragedy of Mabel's unfulfilled marriage bed had worked itself into a dream I had had the night before my divorce court hearing. I dreamt the judge was chastising me for not communicating with Leonard and intimating that the divorce was totally my fault. Judge Cranston was sitting on his bench, fully robed, looking like a crow hovering over a carcass while he asked in a badgering voice why I hadn't told my husband that my toes had never curled.

"If you had cared enough to tell him, maybe you wouldn't be in this courthouse today." His irked tone told me he was on Leonard's side, kindred spirits that they were.

I took the badgering for several minutes and then I stood up in the witness box. In a loud voice, I scandalized the courtroom just as Mabel had scandalized Grandmother. "Your Honour," I shouted, my voice wobbling under the weight of the injustice that was being dealt me. "I could never talk about such things with Leonard. He'd make me feel it was all my fault—something to do with my background. And besides, I didn't want to hurt his feelings. I couldn't even tell him I hated the damn plants he was always bringing home, much less that he never made my toes curl."

Despite having wasted time this morning on wallowing in the past, I was still the first to arrive at the travel agency. The telephone rang before I even had time to take off my wet boots. Unmindful of the soggy footprints left in my wake, I sprinted across the floor to answer it. I was certain that the caller would be someone wanting a hurried departure from the Island.

"Good morning. Sperry Travel. Tess speaking." My voice was cheery. Full of anticipation. The day was shaping up every bit as well as I had hoped.

But the call was not from a prospective client. It was from Frank Clarke, a neighbour from the Cove.

"Tess. Frank Clarke here." Frank's voice was rushed, agitated. "Phoned you at home, but you must've left already." He immediately dropped the reason for his call.

"Got news. Great news. Today's the day!"

My mind struggled to make the transition from the anticipated "get away from the Island" call to Frank's cloaked message: *Today's the day!* I pulled my forehead into a frown, as if squinting the skin on my face would help bring Frank's words into focus.

But Frank was too impatient to let my mind make the transition. "The Writ," he said irritably, as if he shouldn't have to explain what he meant by good news, as if the election call would be foremost in my mind. "'Tis going to be issued today. So 'tis rumoured anyway."

I grasped the side of my desk for support, my body absorbing Frank's news before my mind could. *"The writ!"* I said weakly. *"Today!"* My voice held the tone of a person on death row who has just been asked whether he is ready to be escorted to the electric chair. "Oh no!" I moaned.

"Oh yes, my girl. Today. And on such a devil of a day."

Perspiration began to bead around my hairline and my heart was pounding so hard I could barely hear Frank's voice as he outlined the authenticity of the rumour. He pressed home the point that this was no idle speculation.

"Jack Conway just called. Says 'tis coming today. Said as sure as God made beach rocks it'll be out today." Frank further authenticated the rumour by stating, as I had heard him state before, "Jack's got an in to the Old Man's office, you know. A niece works there. So if he says 'tis comin', 'tis comin'."

He related other bits and pieces of his conversation with Jack, but I had shut off completely. I reached for the Kleenex box on my desk and pulled out a handful of tissues to mop up the terror that was puddling over my top lip and dripping saltily into my mouth.

When I finally spoke it was little more than a moan. "It can't be out today. I'm not ready!"

"What? Talk up, Tess. Seems like you're a million miles away."

"It can't come out today," I repeated. "I'm not ready!" My voice was little more than a squeak.

Frank, unable to hear me clearly, misinterpreted. "*You're ready*! I knew you'd be, girl. That's great! That's wonderful!" His voice was buoyant. "That's what we like to hear."

"I said I'm *not* ready," I repeated again. "It's too soon." By now my voice was so thin it almost disappeared before it reached Frank.

"What?" Frank was certain that he was now hearing me incorrectly.

"You didn't say *too* soon did you? Did I hear you say *too* soon?"

"Oh Lord yes, Frank," I said pleadingly. "It's too soon. I'm not ready." I used excuses, knowing that if I had months, or even years, I still wouldn't be ready to take on the job that was about to come my way with the writ announcement. "Oh Frank," I moaned uselessly, "I'm swamped at work. Just swamped."

Frank refused to dignify my excuses with even so

much as an acknowledgement of them. He bellowed, "Nonsense! Nonsense. If you think you're swamped now, just wait until the election gets under way."

When it comes to politics, Frank is a race horse stomping at the paddock gate, edgily waiting for the race to get underway. But he, himself, never goes through that gate. He insists his talents lie in kingmaking, and while he would vehemently deny ever having personal designs on the throne, he would be the last to deny that he always wants to be the power behind it. With such a bent of mind, it would never occur to him that an election call could come too soon or, for that matter, that a candidate would be unprepared to receive that call.

"He just gave us ten days more than the Act calls for, the Old Man did. Just ten days. Thirty-one days isn't a helluva lot of time to reel in an election," Frank grumbled, as if the lateness of the call was infinitely more important than my state of mind. He paused, muttering to himself, and I knew he was counting days on a calendar. "That's right, girl. Just thirty-one days between the call and the election." He offered reasons for the short notice. "Probably forgot all about us. Out here in the boondocks. Or probably somebody forgot to change the Old Man's calendar. Probably still March in Government House. Who the hell knows?"

Without waiting for my response, Frank veered the conversation to more constructive talk. The issue, after all, was the upcoming election, not whether it was called late or early, or for that matter whether I was ready for it or not. "We've a helluva lot of work to do between then and now, girl," he said, his voice already burdened with the anticipated work load. "A helluva lot of gearing up."

He priorized his list of what had to be done, itemizing what had to be done immediately, followed by what had to be done in the immediate future. But I was no longer listening to him. My mind was occupied with finding a way to tell him that I wanted to rescind my candidacy. After a few minutes of outlining the number of committees he was going to put into place, Frank sensed my inattention and he snapped at me in a schoolmaster's voice. "Tess! You hearin' me?"

For an instant an uneasy silence stretched across the telephone wires and then I blurted out the words I knew he didn't want to hear.

"I don't think I can go through with it Frank. Isn't there someone else ... ? Anyone ... ? It's not too late is it? There's still time?" I stiffened in my chair, waiting for Frank's anger. It came immediately.

"What do you mean you can't go through with it?" Incredulity underlay every word. If I had told him that the sky was falling and it was going to plunge headlong into his house, he would have found it no more absurd.

"Certainly it's too late," he said curtly. "Maybe not legally. You can withdraw any time within forty-eight hours before the opening of the poll, providing you file a declaration with the returning officer. But that's neither here nor there. 'Tis way too late to line up anyone else."

After several seconds had passed and I remained silent, offering no affirmation, no denial, no defence, Frank sensed real trouble. He changed his tack. His voice got softer.

"All candidates feel the same way, girl. You know. Jumpy. 'Tis a big undertaking. And Lord dyin' girl, we need you." He rushed his words, as if there wasn't a moment to lose if he was to bolster my courage. "The Liberal Party needs you. The Cove needs you. And everyone knows that. That's why we nominated you. That's why you won hands down."

But even as I had asked Frank if there was someone else to take over the job, I knew the answer. It was, indeed, much too late to do anything but accept the inevitable, and just knowing that I was boxed into a corner made me impatient with Frank's obvious flattery. "Oh come on, Frank. Cut the slop," I snapped, irritably. "I got railroaded into this and you know it. Is your memory so short that you forget I won by default?" I needlessly reminded him of the situation that had put me in my present position. "No one else wanted the job. Remember! You couldn't find a man who would take on a losing battle, so you settled for me."

Like a child caught in the act of raiding the pantry, Frank sheepishly conceded, "You're right, girl. We did want a man. But now we're glad we couldn't find one. You're what is needed. The women will vote for you, and not, like usual, vote for whatever party their husbands vote for. And the young people will come alongside as well. Times are changing. We need a woman. A young woman. And you're the ticket."

He paused for an instant. When I offered no more protests, he said easily, sensing my acquiescence, "It's nerves, girl. But once the election gets underway, you'll feel different. Everyone's the same. No time for nerves then."

To forestall any mention on my part about the hopelessness of a Liberal win in the Cove and the impossibility of me becoming a member of the House of Assembly, he hurriedly told me that the way the Cove had voted in the past was not our concern now: "It's how they're going to vote in this election that'll count."

To further bolster my courage, he reminded me that he would make a king out of me and for me not to forget that fact. For once I didn't have the strength to remind him of my gender, and that he'd have to settle for making me a queen.

Frank went back to harping about the amount of work waiting to be done to ensure my election to the Newfoundland House of Assembly. He talked about getting me elected as if there was even a thread of hope it would happen. The Cove has always voted Progressive Conservative and nothing short of a miracle would get me enough votes to even allow a return of my deposit—an excruciating embarrassment for any candidate.

"We'll be hopping all over the place in the next few weeks," Frank said confidently. "We'll be busier than a one-armed paper hanger. Busier than a blowfly on a flake loaded with codfish."

He ended the conversation by saying that he would get back to me as soon as he received confirmation of the writ announcement. According to his thinking, it would come before the morning was out.

Now, in the aftermath of that phone call from Frank, I sit in my office, slumped ragdoll-like at my desk, as if someone has removed all of my bones and refilled my body with foam rubber. I reach over, remove the telephone from its cradle, and let the buzz of the busy signal fill the room as I mull over the events that have led to me being the Liberal candidate for the Cove. I am patently aware that I have been the architect of my own fate and that I have no one but myself to blame for my present unpalatable predicament.

Last fall, one crisp October Saturday, I woke up in my St. John's apartment with a deep yearning to visit the Cove. I longed to wander through my house— Grandmother's house, Mother's house, my house— opening a drawer here, fingering a patchwork quilt there, seeing and touching and smelling the bits and pieces of my childhood as I went from room to room. And I had wanted to light a fire in the kitchen stove and let the smoke from spruce logs fill the air with reminders of warm molasses cookies, Uncle Martin's laughter and wet mitts drying over the oven door.

But most of all I had wanted to sit in the parlour, the one room in Grandmother's house that had been out of bounds to me during childhood except on special occasions such as funerals, weddings and visits in the summer from people who came from away. It must have been these very off-limits that made this room so alluring, because the allure certainly wasn't due to its coziness. The windows in the parlour are beach-fronting and the casements were always so loose-fitting that even in mid-summer they let in enough cold air to cover my flesh with goosebumps, making me shiver as if someone had just walked over my grave.

On that October Saturday, I had arrived in the Cove in the early afternoon. I had curled up in the red velvet chair—Grandmother's best parlour chair—to wait for the fire in the kitchen stove to get underway so I could boil water for tea. I sat, tugging the sleeves of my fisherman-knit sweater over my hands. As always, those who began me lined the walls and looked at me out of their oval frames. And, as always, they looked at me disapprovingly—me: Carmel's Tessie, female issue of Carmel Corrigan and her annulled American husband, Ed Strominski; me: the hard-to-manage grandchild of Bertha. Me, the spoiled rotten, but adored niece of Martin.

The ancestors frowned down at me over starched collars and cameo brooches, over handlebar moustaches and tight mouths, their eyes taking in my stretched-out-of-shape sweater, their mouths tut-tutting that I should never haul the cuffs of my sweater over my hands like that no matter how cold I was. And they tut-tutted my wash-faded jeans. In their day no self-respecting young woman wore trousers, and the parlour was certainly no place for such vulgar attire.

In childhood, whenever I had sneaked into the

parlour unbeknown to Grandmother, the eyes of those foremothers and forefathers had followed me about the room. They had followed me as I touched a table here and pulled back a curtain there, and as I picked through the snapshots of Uncle Martin when he was a little boy and of Mother when she went to Boston. And they had followed me as I searched for the one and only picture of my father—the picture that was stashed away from prying eyes because Ed Strominski was *persona non grata* in the Corrigan household.

And those eyes had always followed me charily, waiting for me to trip on a scatter rug or hook my finger in a lace doily and in the process smash something precious—something as precious as the cranberry-coloured glass vase Aunt Bessie had brought home on her one and only visit from Boston. That vase was used every spring for holding purple lilacs. Grandmother said that lilacs made the parlour smell sweet, but according to Uncle Martin they made it smell as if someone had forgotten to bury Poor Mrs. Selena and she had turned to maggots underneath the horse-hair-covered couch. And his saying so took the sting out of Grandmother's tongue the day the vase ended up on the floor in pieces too small to be glued together.

As I crouched in the chair that day last fall, waiting for the water to boil, I mulled over the changes that had taken place in the Cove. Even the land surrounding the Corrigan homestead had changed so much that it barely resembled what I had known in childhood. The hay meadows were now overgrown with wildflowers and weeds and the lane was so filled with goldenrod that I had to trample the heavy, yellow-topped stalks underfoot as I walked towards the house.

And I marvelled that Millie Morrissey's house was barely recognizable. Millie, neighbour and friend dating back to when Grandmother was a girl, had willed her house to her nephew, Frank Clarke, and he had made so many renovations that the house had taken on a completely different appearance.

I had been so preoccupied with my melancholy thoughts, I hadn't heard Frank Clarke's footsteps when he came into the kitchen, and it was his hearty "Anybody home?" that routed me out of my reverie. Even without knowing whom I was welcoming, I shouted back, "In here. In the parlour."

Frank's wife, Rose, had sent him over to invite me to supper, and as had happened on other occasions, there was no way he would return home without having a yes answer for Rose.

In truth, I was always delighted to spend time with Rose and Frank. Their allegiance to the Cove pre-dated mine by at least one generation and I found it pleasant to talk over old times with them. I especially liked to hear them talk about my scampish uncle—the lovable, roguish Martin, whose escapades were known to them even though they were much too young to be his contemporaries.

But on this particular Saturday, Frank was not in-terested in the past. He had recently been elected Presi-dent of the Liberal Association for the Cove riding and his foremost concern was to find a suitable candidate for a by-election, the announcement of which was expected any day.

The problem was that no suitable candidate wanted to let his name stand in nomination. According to Frank, no one with even a half grain of sense about politics had a death wish that strong.—

"Pure political suicide," he exclaimed as soon as we were seated at his kitchen table. "No one will come forward." He tapped his spoon on the edge of his bowl of pea soup for emphasis. "And as sure as I'm sitting here, there'll be an election before fall's out." He predicted the first week in November—before the snow fell and discouraged voter turnout.

He parcelled out background information to acquaint me with the enormity of his problem, feeling that my years in Montreal necessitated a re-hash of Cove politics.

"You see, girl, Ernest Whalen—he's the PC candidate here—he'll be resigning his seat. Any day now. And be God we're all on tenderhooks waitin'."

Frank's voice suddenly dropped, in the manner of one speaking about the dead or the nearly dead. "He's got the cancer, you know. A bad dose of it, too. All through him, they say."

Frank ran his hands over his own body, circling his stomach, liver and kidneys to indicate the extent to which Ernest's cancer had spread. "They say he's as yellow as a turnip, and God Almighty, even on the TV you can see he's so thin he'd frighten the bejesus out of an undertaker."

Then he shivered, as if the prospect of such a death waiting for him, or for anyone, was too horrible to contemplate. "Wouldn't wish that death on anyone, girl. Not even a Tory. And certainly not poor Ernest. Never hurt anyone. All his life he's been like a shit in the ocean, neither help nor hindrance."

Rose, who had probably heard the same conversation dozens of times, told Frank to leave politics alone, or at least give it a rest until he had finished his soup.

"Look here, my son," she said, pointing an admonishing finger at him across the table, "if you don't stop getting so worked up over politics, especially when you're eating, it's your coffin the maggots will be beating a path to—not Ernest's." She added, as a final inducement, "And mark my words, boy, our sickly MHA will be out for the funeral. For the publicity of it. Thin as a slatted fence for sure, but a hell of a lot more alive than you'll be, stretched out in that box, your face rouged up."

Frank had heard Rose's dire predictions on the

state of his health just as often as she had heard his political posturing. He went right on talking, as though she had never spoken, outlining the real reason why no candidates were coming forth.

"No one in his right mind wants to go up against a Tory out here. A nest of Tories. That's what this place is. If you ran a billy goat on the Tory ticket here, it'd win. Probably take every poll."

Frank laughed roguishly. "And I'm not sure they haven't run a billy goat here once or twice. Fer sure Ernest was no better than one." He looked at Rose for confirmation. "Ent that the god's honest truth, me love? Every session he glues his arse to a back bench and never moves it. Never moves anything—not just his arse. Not as much as an eyebrow."

Frank lifted his spoon out of his soup bowl and gestured it towards the television set in the dining room. "Every once in a while we catches glimpses of him on that thing. He sits there like Lot's wife. A pillar of salt. And people who've gone into St. John's for the Sessions says the same thing. He sits there with his mouth closed as tight as a fish's asshole. And that's water tight."

"Oh come off it, Frank," Rose scolded, his vulgarity at the supper table annoying her. "Clean up your tongue, boy, and leave poor Ernest alone. He's not long for this world. Besides, Tess isn't interested in the political shenanigans that goes on out here. Are you Tess?"

Frank didn't give me a chance to reply. "Like hell, she ent," he put in quickly, the aftermath of Rose's rebuke about his vulgarity still edging his voice. "She'd better get interested in what you calls our shenanigans. She has property out here and if she don't want to drive over a road that has potholes you could sink a punchion in, she'd better make sure we elects someone with a mouth instead of an arse."

Rose tossed aside his outburst without taking the slightest offence. She got up from the table and went over to the stove. "I got blueberry pie for us all. Just heating up in the oven. Tinned blueberries, I'm afraid. But the season's gone so we're lucky to have the tinned ones, I suppose."

While Rose was getting the pie, Frank launched into what he termed "the Liberal Predicament."

"You probably know as well as I do, girl, the Liberals out here have always been red-faced about not winning. Especially since most of the Island goes that way. But this is the worst yet. No one to run against the Tories." He shook his head dourly. "A real coronation for them and a laughing stock fer us."

When Rose returned with the pie, she gave me an extra dollop of whipped cream, adding impishly, "Here you go, my love. It'll help the politics slide down."

Frank took no notice of her barb. "Can't get a good man to run fer love nor money," he said, his hand stretching out for the plate with the double wedge of pie. "Everyone is sure they'll even lose their deposit. And that would be the height of embarrassment."

Out of politeness, rather than genuine interest, I suggested several men whom I thought would make good representatives. Frank shook his head over each one. "All has-been's," he said, the turndown of his mouth showing how unsuitable my choices were. "All wash-ups. Re-runs." He curled his lips sardonically. "Not that they wouldn't want to get another kick at the can. Bill Conners would throw his underwear in the ring, not just his hat, if he thought it would do him any good." He shook his head again, this time more emphatically. "No one would nominate him. Jest as well to go without."

Frank took a mouthful of pie and then as if he had pondered the problem into a solution, he said, "Naw girl, what we need is new blood. One good man is what we need. Or better still, one good *young* man who wouldn't be afraid of losing his deposit."

Partly because, like Rose, I was getting tired of Frank's one subject of conversation and partly because his constant harping on finding a *good man* for the job rankled me, I asked him, my tone filled with pretended innocence, "Ever consider looking for a good woman, Frank? A good *young* woman who wouldn't be worried about losing face if she lost the deposit."

"Come off it, Tess," Frank snapped. "Get serious. This is nothing to joke about."

"Who's joking?" I replied, suddenly realizing that indeed I wasn't joking. "There must be plenty of *good* women around here. Women who wouldn't get skittery about losing a deposit."

"That's the truth, Tess, if I ever heard it," Rose cut in eagerly, as if she was glad to have the subject brought out into the open. "There's plenty of good candidates amongst the women, but like Frank said, they'd take a billy goat out here before they'd take a woman." She shot Frank a chastising look. "And Frank is probably the worst of the bunch for that kind of thinking, although God knows I've pestered him to change."

Frank jabbed his fork into his pie with such force that it stood up straight in the crust. He looked first at me, then at Rose and then back at me again. Anger lit up his eyes.

"Fer the lovin' honour of God, will you two stop talkin' bloody horseshit. I'm tryin' to talk a sensible conversation here and all you two can do is act the bloody fool."

"My love, you're the bloody fool," Rose said sweetly. "A bloody fool and don't know it. This is 1970. Times have changed. Besides, it'd be a poor excuse of a woman who wouldn't do a sight better job than Ernest Whalen." She looked at me to join ranks with her. "And Tess don't *you* think it's high time we had a woman in there representing this place? *I* for one would certainly be ready to nominate her."

Frank pushed his plate away and made a move as though he were going to leave the table. "I've jest lost my appetite," he said, looking disgusted and giving Rose a scathing look. "And I think me love, you've been out in the fog too much. It's addled your brain. Or maybe 'tis those pills you've been taking to dissolve yer kidney stones. They dissolved yer brain instead."

He started to get up from the table and Rose laughed and reached over to pull his shirt sleeve. "Sit back down, boy, and finish that pie and stop getting so worked up." Giving me a broad wink, she added, "If you don't watch your mouth I'll drop those pills in your beer and they'll dissolve more than you think. More than you want." She reached over and gave his arm an affectionate pat. "Come on boy, finish your meal. And be man enough to let us have our say."

Reluctantly, Frank sat back down but he made certain we knew he didn't intend to listen. "I'll sit, but I sure as hell won't listen to any more of your bullshit." He immediately proclaimed, as though he were reading from tablets of stone, "Politics is no place fer a woman. She don't have the stomach for it. If I've told you that once, I've told you it a hundred times. Besides, there's never been a woman in politics in Newfoundland and I don't intend to be the first one to put one there."

"Who says there's never been a woman in politics?" Rose returned tartly, her eyebrows arching into a "you don't know as much as you think you do" look. "What about about Mrs. Squires?"

Frank looked from me to Rose, waiting for one of us to enlighten him as to the significance of Mrs. Squires and when we said nothing, he asked irritably, "Who in the hell is Mrs. Squires?"

"Sir Richard's wife, that's who. In 1928," Rose expanded. "She took her husband's seat after he died. Finished for him." She added, taunting, "Come on, Old Man. Don't you remember your history?"

Frank shot her a fiery look across the table and stumbled over a response.

"Of course I remember my history," he bluffed. He built on the information Rose had parcelled out. "And this Mrs. Squires. She didn't know her arse from a hole in the ground. Got in on her husband's coattails. The poor bastard had to die first." He swept the table with his eyes, taking in both Rose and me. "Is that what you want? All of us to die so ye can take over?"

Partly because I was their guest and felt I had to diffuse the heat of the argument and partly because I couldn't think of anything else to say, I tried to lighten the conversation by asking Rose if she knew Mrs. Squires' first name.

"We've always called her Mrs. Squires," I said. "The history books, too, for that matter. Was her name Henrietta or Hortense or something even worse that she didn't want bandied about?"

Rose spoke up smartly. "That should tell you something, shouldn't it? No personal name. The Widow Squires was good enough for her. Why would a woman want a first name anyway when her husband was called Sir Richard?" She shot a cunning look at Frank. "Besides if she didn't know her arse from a hole in the ground, she probably wouldn't be able to remember the name that was christened on her. I'm surprised she remembered she was Mrs. Squires. Maybe she carried her marriage certificate in her handbag. Just to keep her on track."

I burst out laughing and Frank, who felt he was losing the argument, turned on me in a fury. "If you know so goddamned much about politics and history and everything else Tess Corrigan," he shouted, waving his hands wildly, "why don't you put yer money where yer mouth is and run for the Cove." He taunted confidently, knowing full well he would never be called on to make good his words. "You got property here. You've said you consider the Cove your residence. You're entitled to run."

He paused as if he were mentally scanning the Election Act in order to add credibility to his outrageous statement. "Besides, as far as I can recall, the Act states that you can be nominated as a candidate whether or not you're qualified as an elector in the district that nominates you. So there's nothing to hold you back."

"Nominate me and I will," I shot back, willing to match his bluff, equally confident that I wouldn't have to make good my threat. I was sure Frank would choose to eat a flaming torch rather than place the Liberal Party at the peril of a woman.

The instant the words left my mouth the kitchen filled up with silence, the type of silence that takes up every inch of space in a room. It bounced back and forth between Frank and me, ricocheting off our locked glances as each of us waited for the other to back down. Rose quickly ran interference.

"Come on, you two," she said, rushing her words and looking exasperated, as if she were about to separate two fighting cats. "You're always sparring with one another. Never satisfied until you've backed one or the other into a corner."

Again, conscious of being the guest, I said feebly, "Rose is right, Frank. We're just baiting each other again."

Frank sheepishly agreed. "Yes, I s'pose so," he said, never once meeting my eyes. He stuck his fork back into his pie and began eating as though he hadn't eaten for weeks. "Good pie, Rose. Bloody good," he muttered between mouthfuls. For the rest of the visit we made bland small talk, giving the subject of politics a wide berth.

Frank had telephoned early the following Tuesday morning. He said he was calling on behalf of the Cove Liberal Association and asked me if I would let my name stand in nomination for the Liberal candidate. I was in bed and still half-asleep when he called and I was certain he was jesting—retaliation for besting him on Saturday. However, after much explaining and fleet-footed talking, he finally managed to partly convince me that the request was bona fide. He pressed me for an immediate decision—as though I could make such a terrifying decision on an empty stomach; as though I had ever entertained the possibility of having to make such a decision.

"Now *you're* the one with fog on the brain," I had quipped. I was still half-expecting that he'd tell me it was all a joke. "Now you're the one being outrageous. Totally outrageous. You might as well ask me to rob graves. I'd say yes a lot faster." I gave a tight laugh. "And to tell the truth, I thought *you'd* rob graves before you'd ask a woman to run for office."

"The committee thinks you'd make a fine candidate for us, girl," Frank had said immediately after he had identified himself on the phone. There was no lead-in, and he continued to talk as though this wasn't our first conversation on the subject of my possibile candidacy, but merely a follow-up to an earlier one. "They enlisted me to talk you into running."

When I had come awake enough to ask whether he was certain he had dialled the right number, he had laughed self-consciously and began to give me the background on his request.

"You see girl, I was telling the fellows on the committee about the little tiff we had on Saturday ... and well ... and well." Frank stumbled around, groping for the right words to relate verbatim the conversation at the committee table. Most of the members, he said, had seen the joke of our Saturday confrontation, particularly the part about our backing each other into a corner. But not all. Not Greg Slade. Greg thought it was a magnificent idea to have a woman on the ticket.

Frank then explained that Greg was a young lawyer and if the name meant nothing to me it was because his family had moved into the Cove after I left. Greg's law practice was in St. John's, but because his mother had undergone one operation after another since Christmas, he had taken a leave of absence so he would be on hand to look after her. Frank quoted Greg verbatim. "So after the laughing died away, Greg said to the table, 'So what's wrong with running a woman. I don't see anything startling or humorous about that. In fact, I think it's a great idea.' "

Having parcelled out this information, Frank gave a self-deprecating laugh and admitted that at first he thought Greg's idea was preposterous.

"So girl, I said to him right off the bat, 'Greg Slade you may be young and handsome and a smart-enough lawyer, but you don't know much about the world, because everything is wrong with running a woman.' " Frank paused for an instant and added apologetically, "Girl, like I said to you Sunday, I've got nothing against women, but politics is no place for them." Then he added quickly, "But like I told Greg Slade, if there was a place for a woman, you'd be the first one I'd nominate."

I didn't know whether to thank Frank for his backhanded compliment or get annoyed at him for his antiquated thinking, so I said nothing and Frank, hearing the silence and aware that on a long-distance phone call even silence costs money, hurried what was still to be said.

"Girl, I've no idea what this is costing me so I'll

wrap it up by saying that between the jigs and the reels most of the fellows got swayed to Greg's way of thinking and before I realized what I was saying I pipes up and says I'd be one person who'd be glad to sign your nomination paper and Greg said he'd second your nomination and by God after we talked it up some more we came up with enough support to get you on the ticket." He paused to catch his breath and then hurried on. "That's if you want on. Which I really hope you will."

When my answer didn't come immediately, he said impatiently, as though he were watching the second hand on his watch race around and around, "Well, what's your answer? What'll it be? Will you or won't you?"

"Frank, I ... I ... This is ..." I blundered on, trying to get out the words to tell him that what he was saying was so preposterous it didn't warrant an answer.

Frank interrupted, his impatience becoming more obvious, "Will you or won't you?"

After several minutes of trying but still failing to convince Frank that politics was the furthest thing from my mind despite what I had said on Sunday, I gave up and began giving him specific reasons why I was not a suitable choice.

"I'm too young, Frank," I countered, sure that sooner or later he would realize that the lawyer with the avant garde ideas didn't understand the mentality of the Cove. "Who'd vote for a woman who isn't now, or for that matter never intends to be, thirty?"

"Everyone will," Frank retorted with all the zeal of the newly converted. "We need young blood. We've had enough re-runs."

"And I'm divorced. You can't overlook that. In some voters' minds that makes me a scarlet woman. A Jezebel."

Frank acted as if I were offering excuses, not reasons, and my excuses were running up his telephone bill. "If you don't make an issue out of being divorced," he said peevishly, "no one will give it a second thought."

He explained that since I was not in the Cove during my marriage and divorce, most of the people wouldn't even know I had been married, much less unmarried. And besides, didn't my husband come from away? This, he predicted, would surely give me the sympathy edge. His ready answer let me know that my marital status had been analyzed and debated at the meeting, well in advance of Frank's call. His follow-up statement further confirmed my suspicions.

"Like Greg said, he didn't even know you had been married until it was brought up at the meeting. And like he said too, not that it matters."

Frank added his own commentary, his tone more compassionate, "Besides girl, marriages are going on the bum here just as everywhere. No one holds it against people anymore. Like I said to Rose one day, it's a marvel so many couples hang together, not that so many split up. Nowadays you marry a perfect stranger, someone a few months earlier you never even heard tell of. And you have to spend the next forty years with him! It's outrageous." His voice softened. "Now take me and Rose. We went to school together. Her father and my father worked in Buchans mines together and ..." He broke off, flustered over his display of sentiment.

"Aw shit, girl, what I'm trying to tell you is, don't worry about the divorce bit."

When I introduced my job as a problem, Frank tossed aside my concern so cavalierly that I felt stupid for ever having brought it up. "Don't you realize girl, that Sperry Travel would be only too happy to have you involved in an election, especially since you're running on the side of the government."

He outlined the perks. "Think of the political

plum they'll be getting. All that government travel money thrown their way."

That he had to point this out to me should have shown him what a political neophyte I really was, yet when I argued that what I knew about politics could be put in a thimble, he burst out, "Fer the lovin' honour of God, Tess, you were weaned on politics. Martin had you running around the Cove spouting off about Confederation when you were only knee high to a grasshopper."

The mention of Martin's name, unpremeditated though it was, triggered a fast, wily reaction in Frank. It suddenly dawned on him that he had uncovered my Achilles heel. "Wouldn't Martin be some proud of you, girl," he said hurriedly, his voice dipping reverentially. "I can see him now, that scampish smile glowing as bright as a rotten stump in the dark. His Tessie an MHA." He paused an instant at that juncture, waiting for his words to sink in fully before adding the words he knew would clinch my decision. "You know, girl, that'd make him some happy. Yessir, indeed. That would make Martin some happy."

The following day the announcement of my intention to seek nomination for the Cove seat had appeared in all of the newspapers. It further confirmed that I hadn't dreamt that early morning conversation with Frank Clarke.

Tess E. Corrigan has announced her intention to seek the Liberal nomination for the Cove riding. She was born in the Cove and grew up there but is presently manager of Sperry Travel Agency in St. John's. She is active in the Women's Liberation Movement and Big Sisters Organization. If her nomination is successful, she plans to take a leave of absence from her job and to devote herself full-time to the issues pertaining to the Cove riding.

ℰ

For the nomination meeting, Frank had hired the church hall. It would be more precise to say "the acclamation meeting" because mine was the only name on the ticket. Seconds after the applause died down from my acceptance speech, Frank had nudged my elbow and directed me offstage towards the side of the hall where Greg Slade was prying open a window.

"Whew!" Frank exclaimed, wiping the sweat from his face with a wilted handkerchief. "Some christless hot in here. Someone must've stoked up hell." As was his wont in anything to do with elections, he quickly emphasized the positive. "But if that's the price we have to pay to have every man and his dog turn out, I'll pay it." He scanned the hall and noticed that there were almost as many women as men present, so he immediately amended, "I should've said every man and his dog and his wife and his daughter." He gave my shoulder a proprietary squeeze, addressing Greg as he did so. "We've got ourselves a winner here, Greg. She's going to make a good showing for us in this election. Yessir, a real winner for this election."

"You betcha, Frank," Greg agreed, continuing to prop open the window. "But just sealing the nomination makes her a winner in my books."

"This fellow is a real diplomat, isn't he?" I said, turning to Frank. "Covers all bases."

"That's fer sure. And he's some smart, too," Frank replied. "You should see him in the courtroom."

I responded in a tone that Grandmother would have said was half-joking, whole-earnest. "Oh, I don't doubt his smartness for a minute. At least he was smart enough not to let *his* name stand in nomination."

"Now come on, Tess!" Greg rebuked. "You've said

that before and you know it isn't true. You know very well my practice is too new for me to leave it alone for that length of time."

Quickly realizing that by even suggesting the possibility of having to leave his practice for an extended period, he was intimating there was a remote possibility he could get elected, Greg hurriedly amended his words. "Of course, I wouldn't have a hope in hell of winning anymore than anyone else, so I probably wouldn't have to come good with taking time off. But still, there's always that possibility. And you have to be prepared for it."

Frank suddenly became aware of wasting precious moments on trivialities. He hurriedly hooked his arm into mine and told Greg we had to start working the crowd.

"Got to get moving," he said. "Don't want the crowd to thin out before they meet her." He paraded me around the room as if I were a prized heifer that had just taken the blue ribbon.

"Meet our next MHA," Frank gloated as he introduced me to each prospective voter, just as if I had beaten a whole contingent of nominees for the candidacy. We moved from one cluster of people to the other, Frank propelling me onward with one hand, while with the other he mopped his face. His handkerchief was, by now, sopping with perspiration. Under his breath he constantly complained about the excessive heat.

"A boiler room. That's what this is. A goddamn bloody boiler room. Hot enough to cock horseshoes. If I went to hell from here, the change would be so gradual, I wouldn't know the difference."

As I plucked the collar of my dress away from my perspiration-damp neck, I told myself I should have known better than to wear wool, especially a wool sweater dress with long sleeves. The fabric clung to my forearms, midriff and back and whatever other bits and pieces of bare flesh it could locate. I had chosen the out-fit not for comfort but because it was the only suitable yellow dress in my wardrobe. Searching my closet for something appropriate to wear to a nomination meeting, I had become convinced that this was a night that cried out for yellow, especially a soft yellow that reminded me of cows grazing in fields of daisies and of Millie Morrissey's freshly churned butter. Yellow is a colour I associate with good moments and—win, lose or draw—just being nominated as a candidate designated this evening as a good moment.

I had worn soft yellow for my wedding, a V-necked silk coat dress. Leonard had always said that this shade of yellow made my eyes bluer and my hair blacker, but then one day, much later in the marriage, he had turned me totally against yellow by confiding that *she* also wore a lot of yellow. *She*, the para-legal, the woman he would have married had she not taken off for Vancouver with a University of Toronto student shortly before her and Leonard's already-scheduled nuptials. Just moments after Leonard's disclosure of the para-legal's partiality for yellow, I pillaged my closet and carted off a box of clothing to the Good Will depot: yellow sweaters, yellow blouses, even yellow underthings.

However, the day I walked into a dress shop on Water Street—shortly after my return to St. John's—and purchased a pale yellow blouse, I knew I had expunged a few more traces of the pain that was left over from my short-lived marriage and that yellow was once again a colour I could love. And many, many months later I bought an armload of the palest yellow underthings in town. That was the day I learned that the para-legal and Leonard had undergone a fluffy white wedding in Toronto and that Leonard had returned to the fold of Sorenson & Sorenson—which would be changed to Sorenson, Sorenson *and* Sorenson now that Leonard was no longer forced to live in Montreal, where he had exiled himself on account of the jilting. I don't know whether there was any connection between my buying spree and the Toronto wedding, but at the time there had seemed to be a significant one.

I continued to let Frank propel me around the church hall, and before an hour had gone by, my hair was as limp as Frank's handkerchief. Damp strands clung to my ears and forehead and to the collar of my dress.

Earlier in the evening, long before it was time to go to the meeting, I had tried to rearrange my chin-length, straight-cut hair into a fashion more in keeping with the image Frank wanted me to project—knowledgeable, secure, competent. At the very least, he wanted an image in keeping with someone who looked like she knew the difference between a Minister with a Portfolio and a backbencher without one. I tortured the freshly-washed hair into a coil at the nape of my neck à la Grace Kelly and into bun on top of my head à la Audrey Hepburn. Frank dropped in while I was in the midst of my Grace Kelly look, and quipped that I was a dead ringer for those Temperance women who preached that lips that touched liquor would never touch theirs. In the end I accepted failure and let the blunt-cut hair jib out towards my chin in its usual carefree manner.

People filled every available space in the hall. They gathered together in thickets and clumps. Frank continued to manoeuvre me through the crowd, making sure I had an opportunity to say hello, acknowledge congratulations or simply shake hands with each person along the way. Towards the end of the evening he steered me in the direction of a couple who were standing beside a card table loaded down with egg salad sandwiches and marshmallow brownies, compliments of Rose and a contingent from the Women's Liberal Association.

"The Sheppards," Frank said by way of introduction and then launched into an explanation of how

Doug and Margaret Sheppard had come to the Cove from down the bay about three years earlier. "Staunch Liberals. Always were. Always will be." He slapped Doug on the back, a recognition of fellow travellers.

After he got a commitment from the couple to work on my campaign, Frank shunted me forward, giving me aside information on the people who were waiting to meet me. "That fellow in the suit," he said, veering me towards a man leaning up against a wall, "lifelong Liberal." He lowered his voice, "And just to the left of him—that fellow in the windbreaker—he's out for what he can get. If it looks like the Liberals will get in, he'll be a Liberal. If the Commies take over, he'll be as red as a rooster's comb."

For almost two hours we continued to work the room, going from group to group, from individual to individual. Once when we came into a clearing, I mentioned to Frank that I had seen a number of people leaving immediately after my candidacy was acclaimed and I wondered why they hadn't stayed around to offer congratulations, or at least stayed long enough to get a cup of tea.

Frank brushed off my concern, saying brusquely, "Don't worry your head about them. They're ignoramuses. Too ignorant to stay around. Came out of curiosity." He then lowered his head so his voice wouldn't carry and offered a more plausible explanation. "Some are probably Tories, girl. Probably spies. Nosing around to see what kind of strength we have. Hoping to see a split in the ranks so they can reel in a few defectors."

I knew that although my nomination had received almost one hundred percent of the available votes, some of this support had only come at the last minute when it became obvious I was going to be nominated with or without the dissenters' support. And I also knew that Henry Foley had been one of the people who had jumped on the political bandwagon at the eleventh hour, so I shouldn't have been surprised when he left the hall without congratulating me. Yet, I pointed out this insult to Frank.

"Henry Foley left and he never so much as spoke to me. Just turned away when he saw me coming towards him."

"*Him!*" Frank waved his hand derisively towards the parking lot where he was sure Henry was sitting in his car, talking politics with other early leave-takers. "Don't worry your head about him. He's still got a bee up his arse on account yer a woman. Said he'd never mark his X for a petticoat candidate."

Unaware he was painting himself with the loutishness of Henry, Frank added, "But like I told him before this thing got underway tonight, better a petticoat candidate than no candidate."

Petticoat candidate! Frank made the words sound like a vulgarity. All of my reflexes went taut at the insult, unintentional though it was, but to my own astonishment I kept my tongue in check. The pre-nomination Tess Corrigan would have given as good as she was sent. She would have directed a scathing retort arrow-straight at Henry, and in such a way that it would have ricocheted off him to Frank, just to make certain Frank recognized his own vulgar like-mindedness to Henry. But the post-nomination Tess Corrigan had already begun her metamorphosis into her political persona, and this new persona would not let the acid retort escape in public, where it could do considerable harm.

"Well I guess it's up to me to change people's minds about petticoat candidates," I said benignly, and looked at Frank so he could see there wasn't even a trace of a scowl on my face. "And I'll do it in such a manner that Henry won't vote for a man again, even if he has the choice." I chuckled. "Who knows. I might upgrade the image of petticoats so much that even Henry will start wearing one."

Frank shot me an astonished look. "Now you're talkin', girl." He gave my arm a rallying squeeze and let out his breath in exaggerated relief. "Whew! That was a close one. I never intended to let you know Henry's feelings. It just slipped out." He swiped his hand across his brow. "Whew! I thought you'd hit the roof. But you're a real trouper. We were right about you. You're made of the proper stuff for politics. You're already sloughing off the skin of the old Tess."

"You make me feel like a grass snake," I retorted good humouredly, knowing he was right about the metamorphosis that was well underway. I could feel it pulsating throughout my body. No longer did I think of myself merely as Tess Corrigan, former wife of Leonard the barrister and once-upon-a-time branch manager for Sperry Travel Agency. I was now Tess Corrigan, spokesperson for Mary and Bill Rowe, Phil Cleary, Lighthouse Fred, Paddy's Agnes, and on and on down the voter list. Who I was and what I did now affected their lives. Earlier in the evening, something had brought into my mind what Francis Bacon had said about people acquiring power because they think it will give them liberty, but then finding out that the acquisition of power actually means a loss of liberty. Already I was seeing the truth of these words.

"Frank," I said, my voice level and controlled, "I'd give my elbows to be able to tell Henry what an ignoramus he is, but I know that's hardly the way to garner his vote, is it?"

"Not likely, girl," he responded, his shoulders relaxing. He patted my arm again. "That's the way to do it, girl. Roll with the punches. And keep remembering the cause is a lot bigger than that pisspot, Henry." He jerked his thumb toward the door through which Henry had made his early exit. "Or any of the other pisspots for that matter. Just keep remembering that every vote counts."

In true kingmaker style, Frank then tossed the subject of Henry and the like-minded Henrys aside. "But I wouldn't worry too much about them. They're in the bag already. Unless you do something to really rile them up, we've got their votes. They have no choice, girl. They can either not vote at all, and they know that's as good as a vote for the Tories, or vote for you. They'll threaten a lot. You know, posture big. But they'll end up voting Liberal, so 'tis the uncommitteds we have to work on."

I continued to move around the hall under Frank's direction, trying to put the early leave-takers out of my mind as I elbowed through the throng. I tried to convince myself to be content that such a large number had stayed behind. But, like the woman in the Bible who lost a dinari and then fretted over the one she had lost instead of being grateful for the remaining nine, I fretted over the Henrys who had left without speaking to me.

The reality of my successful nomination was confirmed the following day in the *Evening Telegram*. I had read and re-read the article until I could recite it by heart:

Theresa Elizabeth Corrigan, Manager of Sperry Travel Agency, was elected by acclamation at a nomination meeting held last night by the Cove Liberal Association. The President of the Association opened the meeting at 8:30 p.m. and called for nominations from the floor. Corrigan, the only one to declare herself a candidate publicly, was nominated by Gregory Slade and seconded by William Curran. There were no further nominations. Corrigan then spoke to the meeting.

$\wp$

With my candidacy established, my main concern had centred around Ernest Whalen's resignation—when it would occur and who would be his replacement. Both of these questions were answered in February. Again, it was Frank who gave me the news.

I went to the Cove for the weekend—and no sooner had I arrived than Frank came rushing up to the house.

" 'Tis finally happened," he said, huffing and puffing, partly from running up the lane and partly from the excitement of the news he had to impart. "Ernest just packed it in!"

"Well, that's a blessing," I said. "At least he's out of his suffering."

Frank immediately corrected my misunderstanding. "He's not dead, girl. At least not yet. Just resigned his seat."

His tone turned sombre. "But my God, girl, he's not far off. I just had a look at him and he's so thin you can almost see the sins on his soul."

His tone switched again. He had more news to impart. Good news! "And you'll never guess who's going to be stepping up to the gate," he said, a delighted twinkle in his eye. Without waiting for me to guess, he gave the answer. "Randolph Simmons. Dolph Simmons that's who. *Rand Dolph.*" He broke the name into parts, emphasizing each part and grinning impishly as he mimicked Randolph's mother-in-law. "That's how Eileen, the Lord have mercy on her soul, used to pronounce it. Sounded more uppercrust for a son-in-law than 'Dolph'."

Frank's brow furrowed. "Hard to believe," he said, shaking his head in perplexity. "And 'tis going to be by acclamation, I hear. Funny thing. I thought the Tories would have a backlog to pick from. But I s'pose the Walsh's have clout here and they think it will rub off on Dolph." He rolled his eyes to indicate how ridiculous that thinking was. "It'll take one hell of a lot of rubbin' to get anything worthwhile to stick to Dolph if you ask me."

I had been running the name "Dolph Simmons" around in my mind trying to place it, but no recognition came to mind. "Dolph Simmons? I can't place any face to him." I gave Frank a quizzical look. "Should I know him?"

Frank returned my look, pulling his eyebrows into a frown. "Of course you know Dolph Simmons. A bit of a mamby-pamby if you ask me. Never struck me as anyone who could stand up to politics."

I shook my head to show that I couldn't place him in my mind's eye. Frank proceeded to enlighten me. "Sure you know him. Sarah Simmons' husband. She used to be Walsh." Frank raised his eyebrows into a question mark. "Certainly you remember her? Seems to me she'd be your age-mate?" He pursed his lips, reconsidering. "Maybe not. Maybe 'twas her brother? Father Dennis? The *Scarberry* missionary. Probably he'd be the one around your age. You remember Father Dennis don't you?"

I didn't know Randolph Simmons because he had come to the Cove after I left, but asking if I remembered Sarah and Dennis Walsh was like asking Americans if they remembered what they were doing the day President Kennedy was killed. Certainly I remembered both Sarah and Dennis, and I remembered each one in meticulous detail: I remembered Sarah as the painted devil and paper dragon of my childhood. She was the one who knew how to fling arrows with torturous accuracy. And I remembered Dennis as the white knight of my adolescence. The knight who rode off on his steed to the Scarboro Foreign Missions, preferring, it would seem, to make converts of pagans rather than suffer the charms of a Cove damsel—at least, the charms of this Cove damsel. When he made his choice to become a priest, I was so outraged with what I perceived to be illimitable rejection that I entered a convent so I could one-up him by becoming Mother Superior before he got to be Monsignor. But it didn't take long for the shallowness of my vocation to become visible, and I left as hastily as I had entered.

"*Father* Dennis?" I said, forcing Frank to make a leap in thought. "I was sure he'd be *His Holiness* by now. Must've been a disappointment for Eileen."

Frank had no difficulty with the leap. "Well, she died soon after his ordination. Same as Ernest. The cancer. Took her real quick. But I've no doubt she had her heart set on the Vatican for Dennis."

His thoughts took a philosophical turn. "An awful lot of that stuff around. The cancer. But I s'pose something has to get us up above. Tuberculosis used to cart us away years ago. Now 'tis the cancer. I s'pose if they cure that, there'll be a different scourge to take its place. Can't go up without first going down, I say."

He returned to the subject of Dennis. "But Dennis is a well-thought-of priest, Eileen or no Eileen. Certainly well thought of in these parts and I hear in other parts, too. Not the kind who'd break his neck for high office, but I wouldn't be surprised if one of these days he'll make his mark."

Although my path and Dennis' had never crossed in the intervening years, I have had a few brief, "meet in the church vestibule" encounters with Sarah. The last time we saw each other I came away thinking that motherhood had mellowed her, although I could still detect traces of the fire and fight that many times had sent me scurrying back home to Grandmother. Sometimes, I had gone home crying piteously; other times I had retreated, making defiant life-endangering threats that one day Sarah would pay for my misery. But no matter what turn my misery took, I had always been certain that my life would be infinitely more pleasant without the presence of Sarah Walsh.

Sarah and I had been co-owners of a deadly sin: envy. She had envied me because I had a mother in the United States who sent me clothes that were a cut above Sarah's. I had envied her because she had a mother in residence. And a *father* in residence. My father had existed in a nether world of conspiratorial silence. In light of our interconnected and fractious past, it was not surprising that the person I least wanted for a political opponent was Sarah Walsh's husband.

After Frank's frantic phone call foretelling the announcement of the writ and the imminence of an election, I try to get my mind back on the travel agency business. But it is easier said than done. All the while I'm handling telephone customers and setting up travel packages to places far and wide, my heart is palpitating, waiting for Frank's confirmation call. True to his prediction, it comes before the morning is out. He phones me shortly before eleven-thirty. And he sounds even more frantic than before.

" 'Tis already posted in the post office, so they got the word out here fast. You have to get out here, girl. Fast! Tonight, if possible. The ploughs are clearing the roads so you shouldn't have too much trouble."

I wait for the Montreal office to open so that I can let them know what has transpired, and then I telephone Liz, my assistant manager, who has been groomed to take over for me. She tells me she will come in as soon as the roads are open, which she expects will be early afternoon.

In between the incessant phone calls, I try to tie up loose ends having to do with the business. By the time Liz arrives, I'm reluctantly ready to turn the business over to her. I go back to my apartment and pack a suitcase, arrange for the landlord to water my plants and pick up my mail, and by the time I'm ready to leave St. John's the roads have been cleared. However, the driving is still rough so when I arrive in the Cove it is well after dark and I'm too tired to do anything but go to bed. I phone Frank to tell him that we can meet at my place early in the morning.

PART II

I can see Frank's house from my bedroom window. Indeed, from this spot on high ground, I can see all over the Cove. Smoke is already rising from the Clarke chimney, although it is barely daybreak. Knowing Frank, I'm certain he'll be at my house in a few minutes. I rush to get dressed and I barely get the fire going when I see him coming up my lane. He is hurrying as if he is already late and he reminds me of an unbalanced scales of justice—one arm is bowed low under a briefcase filled with campaign material and the other is cupping a container that I know, from last night's conversation, holds Rose's buttermilk biscuits.

I open the door for him and he rushes into the porch, holding out the biscuits. "Rose," he says, nodding towards the baking pan.

I take the biscuits and lead the way into the kitchen. As I pass the stove, I nod my head towards Grandmother's old aluminum percolator that is making comforting noises on the back burner. "Coffee's ready. Help yourself," I say. "And the tea's steeping. Whichever you prefer."

He drops his briefcase on a chair and reaches across the table for a cup.

"I'm already waterlogged from five cups of tea this morning," he says peevishly, as if it is all my fault that he is waterlogged. "I've been up for ages, but waited until I saw the smoke from your chimney."

He goes to the stove to fill his cup with tea and brings it back to the table. "I thought I'd never see the smoke come out of your chimney," he rebukes, and I know if it were up to him we would have an hour's work behind us by now. He absently begins to spoon sugar into his cup, not keeping track of how much he's putting in, nor does he seem to be aware that he is slopping the tea on the table. His movements are quick, uneasy, as if he has something to say which he knows I won't want to hear. A clairvoyant ulcer, that took up residence in my duodenum over the course of my failing marriage, now picks up bad vibrations and forces me to knead that spot of flesh between my breast bone and stomach. The gnawing pain rapidly fans out to other sections of my body.

"Is something wrong, Frank? What's up? You don't seem yourself." Even to my own ears my voice sounds anxious, and it is already escalating to its "prepare yourself for the worst" pitch.

"Oh nothing. Nothing really," he says, offhandedly, but without conviction. He concentrates on stirring his tea as though it is vitally important to make sure every grain of sugar is dissolved. He takes the spoon from the mug and places it heavily on the table, then fidgets with the tablecloth, pressing out invisible wrinkles.

After a few seconds of just staring at the tablecloth, he forces his eyes to meet mine. "Girl, there is something wrong."

He hesitates, the muscles in his jaws tightening. "Well not exactly wrong, I s'pose. No. Not exactly wrong." He stares at the tablecloth again. His glasses shift out of place on his nose and he pushes them back with his wrist.

I jam my knuckles into the soft flesh under my

breast bone to ease the gnawing stomach pains and snap, "What do you mean not exactly wrong? Either something is wrong, or something isn't wrong. Spit it out!"

I am still holding the biscuits and I cross the kitchen to put them in the oven for reheating, but just as I am about to open the oven door, Frank blurts out, "There is something on my mind. I might as well get it over with first as last."

I turn my head towards him and see him pushing his cup and saucer aside, a hangdog look on his face. "I've decided to renege on being your campaign manager," he says, looking my way, but avoiding my eyes. He tosses off sentences just as though they haven't been rehearsed. "It's not really my ball game. Not exactly my cup of tea. You might say, not my forte." Agitated, he mixes and matches his metaphors.

I stop all motion as if someone has pulled the plug on my electrical system. I continue to look at him, my hands clutching the pan of biscuits.

"What!" I say, hoping he will burst out laughing and tell me it is just a joke, although I know from the amount of bile already surging through my duodenum that it isn't.

"Don't even joke about something like that," I chastise, fending off the truth and forcing myself to go to the oven and toss in the biscuits. "I've got enough to deal with, without you pulling funnies on me." I come back and sit down opposite him at the table.

He fumbles with his briefcase, pulling out papers—paraphernalia from past elections. He shuffles the stuff around on the table, pushing some my way, some his.

After a few silent seconds, he says, still not meeting my eyes, "Girl, I'm not joking. I'm serious. Dead serious." His voice is heavy with contrition. He rummages in his pocket for a handkerchief, finds one, and rubs it across his face. "I know I promised. But it would be better for you if I worked behind the scenes. Not front and centre as your manager." His contrition is boundless.

I smell the biscuits burning and get up to remove them from the oven, not caring whether they will be fit to eat or not. My own appetite has bolted and I'm not even marginally concerned about Frank's.

I grab a mitt from behind the stove and open the oven door, remove the biscuits and then slam the door shut. For a lesser slam Grandmother would have sent me to my bedroom. "Better for me! *Better for me?*" I hiss as I plop the pan on the table and fling the oven mitt across the room to land on the couch. "You mean better for *you.*" Desperation raises my voice even higher. "You can't just weasel out now. Not when I'm in over my head. You just can't." I can feel my breath congealing in my chest. Blood rushes past my ear drums with the force of a tidal wave. I see no alternatives. No options. I have to make Frank understand that it is too late for changes, but I can't think of any words that will convince him. I begin pacing the floor like some caged wild thing. I sit back down, then get up again, then sit down again. In a high-pitched voice I say, "I feel as if I have just run afoul of Judas Iscariot or Benedict Arnold. I feel ..." I stop and wave my hand futilely. "Who cares what I feel."

Like me, Frank searches for words and, like me, he isn't able to find the right ones. He knuckles his forehead as if to knead them out of his brain in much the same way as I am trying to knead out the pain of my ulcer. He mumbles contritely, still offering nothing of substance, "Girl, you have a right to be mad at me. I know how you feel. I'd feel the same way. But I'm not doing it to betray you." He shakes his head, vigorously negating my labels. "That's not the way it 'tis atall." He methodically moves his spoon around on the tablecloth, never once looking at me, and begins to explain, his tone self-effacing.

"I jest think that you jest might have a kick at the can now that Dolph's your opponent. You jest might make some headway because they're not dealing from strength with him. So you need the best campaign manager. And I'm much better behind the scenes. I've done a lot of thinkin' and you need an educated fellow up front. These days, with television and newspapers and radios, you need a good education so's not to make a fool of yourself and others. And even if Dolph's a dud, they're still going to throw everything behind him and he himself isn't anything if not slick."

Frank's unexpected humility is unnerving and it leaves me floundering for something to say. On the one hand, I want to negate his own opinion of himself, but on the other I want to shy away from defending him too much, being too understanding. Just as I'm about to say that educated or not, he is still the best campaign manager I know, a pernicious thought flashes into my mind and lodges there. *Frank is having second thoughts about being my campaign manager because he doesn't want to be connected with a sure-fire failure. Dolph Simmons' upcoming nomination has made him see how ridiculous it is for me to be a contender.*

Now I feel not only betrayed, but used. I shout at him, all control thrown aside. "All that humility is so much bunk, Frank Clarke. You just don't want to be hanging on to the tailcoat of a loser, so to save your face you're going to let me be a sitting duck. A Joan of Arc at the stake."

Frank shakes his head, vigorously negating my accusations. " 'Tis not that way at all." He goes back to moving the spoon about on the tablecloth. "It's jest the other way 'round. And 'tis not like I'd be pulling out altogether. I'd work my arse off behind the scenes."

He sounds so sincere, I'm half-inclined to believe him. Still, I continue to badger. "Are you sure it's not because I might make a laughing stock out of you? That I mightn't even get my deposit back?"

If this is the truth, I don't want him to admit to it, and yet I keep pestering for an answer. I crank out reasons why it wouldn't be a wise political move to be my campaign manager, and all the while I'm talking, acid spills into my gut, gouging new craters in its lining.

"You think you'll be branded a loser just because I won't get any votes. What if I hung a sign around my neck, *this big*, printed in large black letters absolving you from any blame for my nomination." With my forefinger, I trace in the air the size of the sign I'd be willing to wear. My mind flits to Hawthorne's Hester and her scarlet letter and I say waggishly, sarcastically, "No, not black. Make those letters red. *Frank Clarke was against my nomination from the start. He has far too much savvy to suggest a woman as a possible MHA."*

"Come off it, Tess. Cut the shit!" Frank retorts, finally fed up with my insults. He snatches up his briefcase as if to leave, but then he realizes that nothing will be accomplished if he walks out now. He settles back. In a tone that, for him, is exceptionally soft, he says, " 'Tis not that I have no faith in you, girl. Not at all. Not at all. 'Tis just that I know politics. And these days you need someone up front with a little more polish than I have. But like I said, I'll work behind the scenes. I'm good at organizing."

I sit back in my chair, the fire taken out of me by Frank's unabashed honesty. After a few seconds to gather strength, I say in a bereft voice, "Without you, I won't stand a ghost of a chance. You're the best."

Frank shakes his head. "There are others. Lots better."

I ask in the same lost voice, "Who? Especially this late. I never would have let you talk me into running if I had any notion that I'd be left high and dry like this."

Frank doesn't reply, but stares down into his

empty teacup. He shuffles the papers on the table, rummaging amongst them until he uncovers two copies of the voter list. He passes one copy to me and he begins scanning the other one, running his index finger up and down the list, not seeming to pause on any one name.

After a few seconds, he tosses the list aside as if he doesn't have any need for it after all. He says, with feigned matter-of-factness, "You won't be left in the lurch. We'll see to that. I talked it over with some of the fellows and we agreed on the type of man that'd be good." He waves his hands like a plane dipping its wings. "Not too old. Not too young. Someone who isn't tied to a job. A bit educated." He reaches over and taps the list with his knuckles as if he is pinpointing a name.

"Bill Curran's a longtime Liberal." He speaks quickly, not wanting me to say anything until he has made his case. "Went to Memorial for a couple of years. Has his own business—the service station. He can always let the help look after it for a short time, or for that matter ..."

"Bill Curran!" I interrupt with horror, dropping my copy of the voter list as though it is in flames. "Surely you're not serious?"

Frank looks baffled. "What've you got against Bill Curran, for god's sake?" He says this accusingly, as though I'm some peevish child needing to be humoured. "Bill Curran is capable. Damn capable. You'd be lucky to get him."

Anger boils up in my throat. It's not only what I have against Bill Curran—although I do have plenty— it's also what I have against Bill Curran being foisted on me without so much as a by-my-leave. It is fast becoming obvious to me that I am being told about this change in campaign manager after the fact, that it had all been decided upon long before Frank scanned the voter list, and that I am not expected to put up any resistance.

"What've I got against him?" I snap, knowing that

even if I hadn't anything against him I would now manufacture something because it is critical that Frank and the others understand I'm no puppet and that I absolutely refuse to be discounted.

"I'll tell you what I've got against him." I hold out my hands and tick off on my fingers Bill's shortcomings, willing to exaggerate them if necessary. "He's a clod. I wouldn't have him spread dogfish on my meadows, let alone be my campaign manager." I curl my lips to show the extent of my disdain. "He's right up there with Henry Foley." I give rapid examples to support my stand, ending with the fact that he calls the opposition a bunch of old women.

Frank gives me a hard, dumbfounded stare and then repeats my complaint. "A bunch of old women! A bunch of old women! And *that* rubbed yer fur the wrong way?" He shakes his head to let me know that my reasoning has always baffled him, but never more so than right now. "Shit, girl, what's wrong with *that*? They *are* a bunch of old women. Their whole Association is filled with old women. Every last man there is an old woman."

I jump up from the table and papers scatter to the floor. "You're just as bad as he is," I accuse, my voice sodden with disgust. I wag my finger across the space that separates us. "And something else about your precious Bill Curran. He's a bloody opportunist." I know I'm on solid ground here because Frank has always said he hates political opportunists as much as the devil hates holy water. "He only jumped on the bandwagon at the eleventh hour. And we both know how he feels about a woman candidate. God knows he's been vocal enough about it. He's certainly made no bones about being an anti-feminist."

For the first time this morning, Frank takes a sharp offensive. He jerks his shoulders erect, ready for battle. Picking up his copy of the voter list, he slams it hard on the table and shouts, "What in hell are you getting at now, Tess Corrigan?" He waves his arms like a wild man. "Don't go all to hell with this women's shit. Don't let it take over yer brains. And don't forget where your bread is buttered. Bill was the one who seconded your nomination. Or don't you remember that far back? He did that when they said it would look better than having me do it, me being your friend and all." Frank draws in a deep breath and gives what he considers to be the last word on the subject. "And as for him being anti-woman, anti-christ, or whatever the friggin' word is, Bill Curran has forgotten more than you ever knew and it would bode you well to keep that in mind."

Pitting Bill Curran's experience against my inexperience is a blow too low for me to accept unchallenged, so I jump up again. "Hold it right there, Frank!" I bark, pointing at him with a pencil. "Bill Curran nominated me because he saw which way the wind was blowing. So let's forget owing dues to him."

Once again I use my fingers for tallying my points. "And as for my lack of experience, you were aware of it when you twisted my arm to let my name stand, so don't go throwing that in my face now. And as for this women's shit, as you call it, you know very well if I were a man you wouldn't even consider selecting my campaign manager without my input. And if I were a man, you wouldn't ..."

I don't have a chance to say what else would be likely to happen if I were a man because Frank interrupts, shouting explosively, "Just one jeesless minute, Tess. *If! If! If!* I'm sick and tired of this *iffin.* If the queen had balls she'd be king."

It seems as though we simultaneously realize that our conversation is becoming outrageous and that our infighting can only be destructive to our cause. I slump back into my chair. From the abashed look on Frank's face I can tell that he, too, is dislocated by our fighting. I reach over and touch his sleeve. "This will never do, will it?"

"You're right, girl," he says, chastened. "This will never do." He gives my hand a reassuring pat. "We've got to pull together." Frank is even willing to be conciliatory. "And in hindsight, girl, I can see why you'd be galled not to be asked your opinion. We just never thought." He rubs his face as if to rub away the weariness. "So much to do and so little time."

Frank's voice now turns gruff, because he is more comfortable with gruffness. "So 'tis back to the drawing board. We need to get you a campaign manager." This time when he picks up the voter list he actually reads the names. He stops abruptly. "I know someone. Certainly I do." His tone holds surprise. "I don't know why I didn't think of him before. Not on this list I s'pose. Voted in St. John's last time. Greg Slade. What do you think of him?"

I pause for only an instant. "Of course! Greg Slade. I think he'd be terrific." My enthusiasm is honest. Whenever I have attended meetings with Greg, I have always been impressed by his ability to analyze situations and to cut through problems. "I think Greg would make a splendid campaign manager. He has ideas. And loads of energy."

I recall what Greg said on nomination night about his practice being new and needing his attention. "But would he want it? What about his practice? He said it needs his steady attention."

Frank brushes this obstacle away. "Hell's flames, girl. Shouldn't be any problem at all. It'd just be for a few weeks. Not like he'd be running for MHA. It wouldn't be long-term. Just for the duration of the campaign."

"Yes, that's true," I acknowledge, anxious to believe that Greg would consent to take on the job. "Perhaps he'd be willing to give up a few weeks. A few weeks wouldn't take too much away from his work."

Now it is my turn to be conciliatory. I want Frank to have the honour of asking Greg. "We should get to him right away. Why don't you call him since you know him better than I do?"

Frank doesn't even hesitate. "Naw. I think it'd be best coming from you. You're the candidate. But like you say, I'd try to get hold of him right now." He nods across the kitchen towards the black, vintage telephone I have never bothered to upgrade. "No time like the present."

As if in answer to Frank's question, the telephone rings and when I answer it, Greg's voice greets me. In the same circumstances, Grandmother would have said, "Speak of the devil ..."

"Good morning Mademoiselle Candidate!" Greg's voice is buoyant. "Just wanted to let you know that I've a real knack for putting posters on fences and telephone poles. And I can lick envelopes with the best of them."

I look towards Frank and mouth *Greg Slade*, giving both names, as if we know several Gregs and need to distinguish one from the other.

"Good stuff," Frank hollers loud enough for Greg to hear. "Ask him if his ears are burnin'."

Hearing Frank's voice, Greg is embarrassed at having interrupted a meeting. "I'm sorry, Tess. I didn't realize you'd be having a meeting set up so early."

"It's not really a meeting," I quickly assure him. "Just Frank. You know how the saying goes. Mad dogs and Frank Clarke get up at the crack of dawn."

Greg laughs and adds, "Especially when there's an election brewing."

If he heard Frank's remark about burning ears, Greg fails to pick up on it. Instead he immediately gets to the real purpose of his call. "Don't want to encroach on your time," he says, hurrying his words. "Just want to forewarn you that Jim Patterson's in a snit because you didn't rent that dump of a building of his—the one down by the wharf—for a headquarters. He's saying you're renting your own house to make a bundle. He says several people told him you're getting a hefty daily rate."

"But that's preposterous!" I retort, shocked that such bald-faced lies have spread so fast. "I'm not getting a red cent for this place. I'm using it for convenience and to prevent just this sort of patronage thing from happening." I let the stridency dwindle from my voice and state the obvious. "But you know that."

"Certainly I know that," Greg says emphatically. "And Jim probably knew it too. At least if he didn't, he knows it now because I took great pains to enlighten him."

Greg sounds disgusted with such blatant pettiness. "Jim's just bent out of shape because he hoped to haul in a bundle himself." He tells me he explained to Jim that I agreed not to charge rent for my house so we could free up some more money for the campaign. Jim, however, refused to believe a word of what he was told.

Greg advises that a little brush-fire dousing is now in order. "As soon as you get a little more organized there, you should try and reach him. You know what a big mouth he has. He could lose us votes. We've got to pacify him somehow." Assuming Frank is my campaign manager, he adds staunchly, "I'm sure Frank will know how to deal with him. He's known him for years. Knows what he's like. Like my mother says, Jim Patterson has a tongue like the clapper in a cow's bell—always flapping."

I know this is the time for me to inform Greg of Frank's defection and to ask if he would be willing to take on the job, but because I don't feel up to another rejection, I dodge the problem by extending the present conversation. "Thanks, Greg. We'll get cracking on that even *before* we get a little more organized. I think it's vitally important to quash that rumour." I chuckle. "Good thing I don't have any relatives. They'd be saying I have them on the payroll."

I glance over at Frank and see that he is impatiently rubbing the corner of the kitchen table with the palm of his hand as if he is trying to rub the wood smooth. There is a "get on with it" look on his face. But I ignore his frowning and impatient squinting, and continue to talk incidentals, telling Greg about our makeshift headquarters, about how we've kept the parlour out of bounds as well as the upstairs portion of the house.

"Frank's going to get a lock that latches and put it on the parlour door because the one that's there now doesn't work and the door is always wide open. And he's going to put up some sort of makeshift door at the bottom of the stairs. He says just saying the rest of the house is out of bounds won't be enough."

"Good thinking," Greg agrees easily, and adds, "You and Frank certainly make a good team. You're very fortunate to have him. No one could get a much smarter campaign manager than Frank Clarke." Greg laughs self-deprecatingly. "Just listen to me telling you what you already know."

I laugh too, a surface laugh that rings hollow even to my own ears. "That's true. I do know that." For Frank's benefit I repeat Greg's words. "You're right, Greg, I couldn't get a much smarter campaign manager than Frank Clarke." I then take a deep breath and plunge headlong into the possibility of another rejection. "But unfortunately he doesn't want the job."

"What? What?" Greg sounds totally bewildered. "Say that again. You can't be serious. You must be putting me on. Frank and elections go hand in glove. He's the best there is."

I grab at straws. "Greg, maybe you can talk some sense into him. He just dropped this news on me a few minutes ago. In fact we just got through talking about it when you called." I look Frank's way. "Or fighting about it would be more precise. I've called him every kind of traitor in the book, but he still won't take on the job. Says he'd rather work behind the scenes."

Screwing up my courage even further, I forge ahead. "He says *you'd* make a great manager. That's why he asked if your ears were burning."

"*Me?*" Greg's bewilderment turns to astonishment. "*Me?* Be your campaign manager? Holy Geez! Frank suggested *me?* To replace *him?*"

"He says you're the best." I rush my accolades, hoping to swing his answer. "He told me this morning they don't come any better. Says you are better equipped for the job than anyone he knows." My breath is short by the time I've finished. My hands are perspiring. I throw some books off a chair and sit down. "For the love of God, Greg, hurry up, say yes. I can't stand any more of this suspense."

But Greg won't be rushed. "I'm flattered all to hell, Tess," he says, reverting to his calm, controlled self, "but I've got no experience. I've never worked a campaign before."

"And neither have I," I interrupt quickly, not wanting to hear his list of sound reasons why he shouldn't take on this job. This is not the moment for common sense and in-depth reflection. If it were, I'd concede defeat to Dolph Simmons right now. I add encouragingly, "So we'll be babes in the woods together. And if we haven't experienced the ecstasy of success, we haven't experienced the agony of defeat either." I pause, expecting Greg to respond with some quip about knowing the agony of defeat soon enough if the two of us take control of this election, but only silence reaches me. Perhaps he can see nothing humorous in abject failure.

My heart begins to thump so furiously, I wonder whether I'll be able to hear Greg when he does get around to giving me his no answer. Unconsciously, I have been holding my breath for the past several seconds and my ribs rebel from the pressure. I exhale loudly, the phone still clutched tightly against my ear. I can feel my face arranging itself into a tired, worn look. Already I'm wishing I were back at the travel agency making up vacation packages for blue-haired ladies in flowered crimpline. I'm even wishing that I, myself, were one of those ladies and that I was heading off to Florida in my elasticized waistband slacks with my straw hat, crushed from last year's trip to Hawaii, strung to my tote bag.

I squeeze my eyes tight and for a few seconds concentrate very hard, hoping that through telepathy I'll be able to infuse Greg with a desire to tackle this job. When I do open my eyes again I glance towards Frank. He is staring at me, and this time his face is wearing a "what's the bottom line" look. Just when it seems I have been waiting for an eternity, I hear Greg's voice, and it is more resigned than exuberant. "It's a deal, Tess. But I'm no saviour. No miracle worker. I can't raise Lazarus. You have to understand that. And I can't make Grits out of Tories."

Relief surges over me and my body folds itself even deeper into the chair beside the phone, as though it wants to remain there forever.

"Thank you Greg. Thank you," I whisper, searching for my voice. "I'll appreciate this forever." My strength returns, and in the aftermath of so much tension, I become high-spirited. "This day you shall be with me in Paradise, my son. Or in other words, I'll never forget you for this. And I promise you I won't expect miracles. You won't be called on to rout Lazarus or anything of that magnitude."

Frank, hearing my grateful babbling, shouts across the room. "What do you mean we won't expect miracles? We'll want him to turn a few barrels of brackish water into wine right now so we can peddle it around the Cove to jig a few votes."

Greg hears this, and tells me to tell Frank that we won't be needing liquor. We'll mesmerize them with the truth instead. After I end the conversation, I remain seated, rooted to my chair, feeling every bit as woebegone as I did the day Frank called to tell me that the writ was going to be issued.

§

Frank has made lists and lists of voters who have offered to serve on different committees, and once we have these in place we set about arranging the downstairs portion of my house so that it is more in keeping with the needs of a political headquarters. Frank takes up daytime residence in what once was Grandmother's pantry/storage room, and from here he oversees all aspects of my campaign. He is in shouting distance of the dining room, which Greg and I share. The big, eat-in kitchen has been designated as the "drop-in room" and it is always filled to overflowing with people, volunteering for work. Some come to ask about issues; others come just to mill about, looking for a warm place to kill time. The coffee pot and teapot are constantly ready on the back of the stove, thanks to the Women's Liberal Association, and styrofoam cups are spread out hither and yon over the table. It is almost impossible to find a sheet of paper that isn't splotched with coffee or tea.

The campaign posters (Elect Corrigan! Vote Liberal! Say Yes to Dedication!) have been allocated to the large back porch so they can be picked up by anyone willing to prop them up in their yards or nail them to a fence or pole. However, the posters never seem to stay in the porch. It's as though they can move about under their own power and we find them lolling all over the place—always in someone's way. Frank keeps pushing them off his desk and cursing whoever is responsible for seeing that they stay in their own space.

My office is at one end of the dining room table; Greg's is at the other. With his light-sensitive glasses and crew-neck sweater, Greg looks as though he would be more at home on the ski slopes than pondering the hopeless and hapless fortune of a Liberal candidate in the Cove. But every time I look at him and start to think that he is too young for so much responsibility, I have to remind myself that I'm even younger. To bolster my courage and quell my fears, I recall what Robert Louis Stevenson said about politics—it is the only profession for which preparation is thought unnecessary.

However, what both Greg and I lack in experience, we make up for in zeal. Between us we have worn the soles and heels from three pairs of shoes and bruised our knuckles from knocking on doors. And the campaign is only in its infancy. This morning Greg is finalizing a trip to the hospital, and trying to arrange for people to make buttermilk biscuits so we can have tea with the ambulatory patients in the hospital's sunroom.

As I'm thinking that Greg and I must surely be the two most unlikely people to be caught up in an election, a campaign worker comes into the dining room and sets a pile of scratch paper before Greg like a dish before the king. Greg's face lights up. These bits and pieces of paper hold the answers to a telephone survey on the question of issues: what issues would you like to see your candidate promote?

"Issues," Greg says somberly, holding his hands over the pieces of scratch paper as though he is anointing them. "That's what's going to win or lose this campaign. Issues! We've got to make absolutely sure we're flogging the right issues. Should've done this survey before now instead of just assuming issues."

He picks up the papers and scrunches them in the palm of his hand and then lets them dribble onto the table. "What's the use of a campaign without issues!" He reminds me of Alice in Wonderland. *What's the use of a book without pictures or conversation?* Absentmindedly, he lifts a displaced campaign poster from underneath his elbow and places it behind a chair by the wall. From my vantage point, I can see my cardboard likeness peering out, sombre and pensive, from between the chair's legs. I look like a child who has been punished for an infraction of some rule important only to adults. Several photography sessions went into the making of these posters—an assignment that severely challenged the mettle of the young Liberal photographer. I had to look taller and wiser and older and kinder than I am. And above all, I had to look trustworthy. As Frank said, I must be made to look like "a sincere, honest fellow with enough smarts to get the job done."

Although the posters have been out in the community for less than a week, already they have been bent, folded and mutilated. My face has run the whole gamut of the Marx brothers. Moustaches, glasses and hats have been pencilled in. On one poster, in the white space underneath my slogan someone has scrawled, "A woman belongs in the kitchen; not in the House (of Assembly)." A villainous handlebar moustache was added to another one, with the question *"Would you buy a used car from this woman?"* printed below. It is a full-time job for volunteers to find and replace the defaced posters. I pretend I don't mind the added slogans and the defacing, but the truth is, I cringe every time one is brought to my attention. I have to keep steeling myself against Frank's earlier prophecy that women don't have the stomach for politics.

"Issues!" Greg says again, forcing me to concentrate on the present. "We'll stand or fall on issues." He nails home the importance of his statement by letting more papers rain down on the table.

I bob my head in agreement although I'm not certain what he's talking about. I feel like a charlatan. I haven't been deeply enough connected with Newfoundland during the last several years to know which issues are important to the province, much less which ones are important to the Cove. So far, I've managed to camouflage my ignorance by letting Greg do most of the talking when we go door-to-door.

Greg beckons me to pull my chair closer. "We've got to talk these over right now," he says, raking the crumpled issue papers towards him. I pull my chair around to his side of the table, and because some fragment of my mind has still lingered on *Alice in Wonderland*, I mumble, "The time has come the walrus said, to talk of many things, of shoes and ships and sealing wax, of cabbages and kings."

Greg rounds off the quotation, improvising as he goes along, "And why the sea is boiling hot and why issues are the things."

He opens up one of the scraps of paper as gingerly as if he is taking the lid off Pandora's box. He reads it and then passes it over to me.

"Well just as I expected," he says matter-of-factly, as he tosses issue after issue my way. "Work! That's the number one issue. At least we've been on the right track in flogging that one." He then justifies the time spent on the telephone survey. "But even if we don't come across any new issues, it will make us feel more confident flogging the old ones. I'll bet you a nickel most of these papers say work. Especially work for the young. With the rumour of the base closing down completely, things look gloomy around this place."

He quotes statistics he read recently in an article about the young people in Newfoundland leaving for the Mainland. "Youth drift" had been the thrust of the article, and Greg agreed fully with its contents.

"That's what's happening in Newfoundland," he

says, his tone damning. "Not just in the Cove. All the young men heading for Toronto looking for work and ending up on welfare, or worse, on the streets. And if they don't go to Toronto, they go to Vancouver or Alberta. Some of them get lucky and manage to get enough work for their passage back home. God knows what happens to the others."

Greg doesn't mention the young women, so I'm curious about what impact the lack of work has had on them. "What about the young women?" I ask. "What do they do? Do they leave, too?"

Greg shakes his head. "Some. Not all. Between nursing and teaching most of the educated girls manage to find work. The others ..." Greg purses his mouth. "Well, they end up married, having babies and being left behind while the husband hits the road."

It suddenly strikes me that, although it may appear that work—or lack of it—is the main issue, this really isn't the case. The real issue is education, or more precisely, the lack of educational opportunities in the Cove. Since I started campaigning I have noticed that there are a number of young people lolling about, as though they are just aimlessly putting in time, and I have often wondered why they aren't occupying their time more gainfully. I speak my thoughts to Greg. "I see a lot of young people hanging around the garages and the stores. They seem to be just killing time. If there isn't any work for them, why aren't they off at vocational school somewhere?"

Greg peers at me over his glasses and gives me an exaggerated look. "Come out of your ivory tower, Tess, my girl. Get real. There's not enough vocational schools to hold everyone. And even if there were, they're in St. John's and Corner Brook." He adds cryptically, "Board to pay. Clothes to buy. Who can afford that? Especially if the householder isn't working."

From my naive perspective the answer to the

problem is as clear as the problem itself. "So then we have to get a vocational school out here. With all the outlying villages, there'd be plenty of students." I say this with such a feeling of *fait accompli* that Greg leans back in his chair and chuckles heartily.

"What's so funny?" I ask defensively. "I can't see anything outrageous about educating these young people so if they have to leave, they'll at least be qualified to earn a living."

Greg laughs even more heartily. "Oh Tess of inflated faith," he says, raising both arms in the manner of God bestowing a blessing on mankind. "Let there be a technical school in the Cove and there will be a technical school in the Cove."

Seeing my look of indignation, he drops his arms to the desk. "Tess," he says, instantly all sober cynicism. "The Cove is not the most popular place with the Old Man. I can't see him handing out money for a college out here." He waves his hands to take miracles into account. "Even if miracles were to happen and you do get elected, you'll still just be a voice crying in the fog. Or hollering from a back bench."

I abruptly rupture his prophesying. "I don't give a damn whether I get elected or not," I say, my voice rising to such a pitch that it surprises even me. "No matter who the member is, it doesn't alter the fact one iota that these young people need an education."

I continue on my soapbox, my voice now more impassioned than ever. "We're wasting all that potential! Squandering minds!" Although I'm sitting down, I feel as though I'm stomping around the room, hammering home point after point. I slap my right fist into the palm of my left. "For God's sake, man," I say, as though I'm addressing an opponent rather than a kindred spirit, "this youth drift the politicians talk about is not some offshore fog that gets blown over to Toronto or Alberta;

it's our young men and women. And we're sending them away without half enough survival skills."

Suddenly, Greg bangs the desk with the palms of his hands like a mother seal slapping the rocks with her flippers. He pretends he is in the House and applauding the maiden speech of a fellow Member. "Bravo! Bravo!"

He looks towards the pantry door and shouts, "Frank! Frank! Come here! There it is!" He sounds as exuberant as if he had just come upon the lost city of Troy. "There's the passion you told me was in her if we could only get it to surface. Well, it surfaced. The old Martin hellfire and brimstone you told me about. It's here." He turns back to me. "Good God, girl, we've got to keep this fire going until after the election. Got to keep you riled up till then."

Frank comes out and pats me on the shoulder, a broad grin on his face. "I heard you. Could have heard you all the way over to Red Island if the wind was blowing right. You tell 'em, girl. Give 'em hell about all that good stuff. About demon rum and neglected youth and wild wild women."

I irritably shrug off his hand, peeved that they are both making fun of my earnestness. "Stop poking fun! The both of you. And I don't give a tinker's dam whether I win this election or not, I'm still going to fight for a vocational school out here!"

"Go Tess, go!" Greg shouts. "Fight, girl. Fight! All the better to become a Member of the House of Assembly, says the fox to Goldilocks." He shuffles the issue slips that are heaped on the table and cools off my ardour with common sense. "But you can't be known as the 'one issue candidate.' You've got to realize one issue won't do it. You have to say, 'Oh Grandma what big potholes you have in the roads out here. But just wait until I get elected and I'll fix them.' And you have to say, 'We only have half enough beds in the hospital. But just wait until I get elected and I'll get more.' And you have to say, 'There's no reason why we can't have a senior citizens' home here like they have in other communities only half the size of the Cove. But just wait until I get elected and I'll have one built.' " He holds up a piece of paper. "And you have to have an answer for Mrs. O'-Rourke who wants a job in the government for her lazy, layabout son, Kevin, who was born with his arm bent at the elbow asking for handouts."

Suddenly, as if reiterating the issues reminds him of the impossibility of the task ahead of us, Greg lets the paper drop to the table. He says, in a voice that already seems battle-fatigued, "Oh God Tess, I don't know why we got ourselves into this racket. I'm worn out already."

At the end of each day we come together over a supper that is supplied by the Women's Liberal Association. We meet to discuss policy and strategy and to outline the next day's agenda. Greg and I always bunch our papers into the centre of the dining room table to make room for the dishes and for Frank, who chairs the meeting. As well, we make room for newcomer Anthony Henderson, who has been given the double duty of scouting for issues and of finding places for me to visit and people for me to talk to, and for Bill Curran. Bill was brought in by Frank to look after publicity and he shares Frank's pantry, although he does both with poor grace because he believes he deserves a room to himself and considers looking after publicity a comedown when he really wanted to be campaign manager.

Greg and I have never fully understood why Frank decided to involve Bill Curran in committee work because Bill has certainly taken no pains to disguise his disgruntlement over our choice of Greg for campaign manager. We surmise his presence in the pantry has something to do with old loyalties and past favours. Although we both suffer from Bill's thinly-concealed resentment over our usurption of his rightful position in this election, Greg bears the brunt of it. From time to time the cold war that exists between the two of them breaks out into border skirmishes—altercations, I might say, that Frank takes great pains to ignore. On a couple of occasions, there have been mix-ups between Greg's agenda of meetings for me and Bill's public notices of these meetings. One such mix-up took place last Sunday. I was supposed to be attending a church bazaar at the same hour as I was scheduled for a coffee party in a home. I managed to keep both appointments, but not without considerable fluster.

When we are traipsing around the Cove en route to here or there, Greg and I speculate that these mix-ups are sabotage attempts by Bill, made just to aggravate us. However, we always quickly squelch such thoughts, finding it hard to believe that "Give me Liberal or give me death" Bill would take a chance to scuttle the cause on such petty grounds. Sometimes, though, when we get so tired that we resort to black humour, we tell each other that Bill is indeed fiddling with the time schedules and he is the one who is responsible for the double bookings and that he is also the one who is going around the Cove defacing my posters, giving me Hitler moustaches and vampire teeth.

Frank would have the opposition believe that our headquarters operates like a scene from Ozzie and Harriet—all for one and one for all—even though with each passing week it gets considerably more difficult to carry off this facade.

"At all costs a united front," Frank charges our

group each evening, as religiously and as constantly as the church bell that rings out the *Angelus* when the clock strikes six. "We must always maintain the outward appearance of closed ranks." As he says this, his voice gets thick with fervour and his tightly closed fist demonstrates the extent of the solidarity we must project.

"Not by word or action should we let them know we're not as tight as *this*." He holds clenched fist above his head, his knuckles pressure-white.

Hardly a meeting goes by without the matter of how best to conduct the campaign surfacing for discussion. Frank believes in personalized canvassing, going door-to-door, attending the card parties that are held in the church hall, and standing in the vestibule of the church each Sunday, shaking hands with all and sundry. Once in a while he is not beneath wishing that some of the old people, who he says are "barely dodging the undertaker," would up and die during the campaign so we could be there to offer sympathy and consolation.

Greg is strongly in favour of directly involving the youth in the campaign. He says that today's youth are capable of making up their own minds and they won't be hidebound by the Grandfather syndrome. He wants each of us to find jobs that can be done just as easily by an inexperienced young person as by one of the old hands and he constantly infuriates Bill Curran by giving out pamphlets and posters to the young people who come by the headquarters looking for jobs to do.

Bill favours locking horns publicly with Dolph Simmons in a debate, and he is itching to get one underway.

With the exception of Bill, we all try to incorporate each other's ideas into the campaign strategy, but so far we have shied away from a public debate. Lately, though, as soon as we sit down at the table for our evening meeting, Bill brings up the subject of debating. He steeples and un-steeples his hands as he pontificates on the merits of demolishing Dolph within full view of every voter in the Cove. It annoys me that I'm so vulnerable I can be flattered by knowing that someone—even if that someone is the likes of Bill Curran—thinks I'm capable of demolishing anyone in a political melee. In the deep recesses of my soul I'm convinced I'll end up making a fool of myself in a debate. Still, fear aside, when we gather for our evening meeting and Bill asks me how I think I would fare in a one-on-one debate with Dolph, I'm astonished to hear myself saying that I'm ready and willing to take on Dolph just as soon as something can be set up.

"Certainly I'd be willing to debate with Randolph," I say, hoping the fear in my voice will pass for fervour. "I'll take him on any day of the week."

The words have barely escaped my lips when Bill announces he already has everything arranged. He eagerly outlines the format the debate will take. Questions will be garnered from the floor and then placed in a hat. Each candidate will select a question by the luck of the draw method. As if my confidence is in need of deflating, Bill tells me that Dolph is going around the Cove bragging how he is going to bury me in a debate. Apparently, he is tallying up my shortcomings, predicting my voice won't carry, my inexperience will betray me and worst of all—or best of all if you are Dolph—my years in Montreal will show up in my accent. "Come from away" will be stamped on me, and it will be every bit as damning as a scarlet letter. According to Dolph, this debate is an opportunity for me to betray myself for the foreigner I am—or the foreigner he would like people to perceive me to be.

Greg is dubious about the debate, especially about its format. He discusses the pros and cons of the draw from the hat arrangement, and wonders whether there is some way we can increase the odds of my getting favoured questions. Although Frank would prefer that the whole notion of debating would go away, he is pragmatic enough to realize that we no longer have the option to refuse, especially now with Dolph's swaggering remarks about his eagerness to confront me in a public debate—if only I had the courage to accept his challenge. Only Dolph doesn't say "courage." His words to describe my cowardice are much more graphic and Bill restates each one with relish. Frank is convinced the Opposition will have a field day if I don't consent to this head-on confrontation. He says we can't afford to shore up Dolph's remarks that I don't have enough spleen to publicly confront him.

As with my nomination, the newspaper confirms the reality of the debate:

COVE CANDIDATES TO DEBATE
Candidates running for office in the upcoming provincial by-election in the Cove riding say they will be sponsoring a "Meet the Candidates" evening that will take the form of a public debate. The date, time and place of this meeting will be announced as soon as scheduling can be arranged.
Both candidates, Tess E. Corrigan, Liberal, and Randolph Simmons, PC, will be given the opportunity to speak for four minutes at the beginning of the evening and they will then respond to written questions solicited from the audience prior to the beginning of the speeches. The questions will be placed in a hat and will be drawn at random by the speakers.
Each candidate in turn will draw a question from the hat and will have three minutes to respond to the query. The other candidate will then be entitled to a one-minute rebuttal. There will be no direct questioning from the audience.

"I feel like one of those Greek virgins they used to sacrifice to appease capricious gods," I tell Greg as I shove the *Evening Telegram* across the dining room table towards him. "It's all there in black and white."

Greg laughs and then immediately corrects my perception. "There you go, romanticizing again," he chortles, picking up the newspaper. "You'll be more apt to look like one of those Christians who supplied lunch for the lions. No ceremonies in white robes with rites and rituals in this debate. Just over the side and into the gullet of a lion—or in this case, into the wily snare set by Old Dolph."

"It's easy for you to make jokes," I retort indignantly. "Just see how humorous you'd be if you were the one pulling out the questions and everyone sitting back waiting for you to foul up."

Greg sobers instantly. "Just kidding, Tess, old girl. Just kidding." He reaches over and touches my hand, a "not to worry" smile on his face. "Besides, girl, we'll have you so well prepared for that debate Old *Rand Dolph* will come away feeling like Nixon did when he debated Kennedy—wishing he had never broached the subject."

Frank, overhearing our conversation from his desk in the pantry, shouts out, "That's a fact, girl. We'll have you so well primed you'll know the ins and outs of everything that's gone on. All the skullduggery." He leaves the pantry to come into the dining room, and begins outlining the bits and pieces of knowledge that they intend to force-feed me.

"If they want to know things like how much money the Government loaned to Ocean Harvesters you'll be able to tell them." His voice takes on a sardonic tone. "But let's hope they don't open up that kettle of fish." He outlines other likely subjects that may surface. "And you'll be able to tell them how much money was loaned to Bonavista Cold Storage." With a flourish of hands, he concludes, "Even if they ask you how much the Old Man paid for the pisspots for his place up there on Roche's Line, you'll have it down to the penny." He chops the air with his hand, index finger wagging my way. "And remember this! Always hammer home the whopping sum of money that was just approved for education. That's something we have in our favour. And be sure and let it be known that you intend to get some of that booty to get a college going out here. Get that in wherever you can. And shit, girl, it doesn't matter a shag if it fits or not. Just work it in somehow."

℘

When I come downstairs on the morning of the debate, Frank is already in the headquarters.

"Well, girl, this is *it!*" he says as soon as I enter the kitchen. "This is the day!"

He is standing by the stove, pouring himself a cup of tea. Although it is only six o'clock, he looks like he has been at work for hours.

"Yeah, this is *it* alright," I repeat, yawning and feeling so tired it seems more like the end of the day than the beginning. The old aluminum percolator is on a back burner of the stove and Frank fills a styrofoam cup with black, left-over coffee and hands it to me, admonishing, "Get this into you right now. I told you to sleep last night so you'd be at your best this evening."

Before the debate was set into motion, I had thought my head was filled to the point of bursting with snippets of political facts and figures, and with issues, issues, issues. But I hadn't realized then how much more was going to be crammed in. For the past several days, we have met every morning at seven o'clock for the sole purpose of grilling me on issues, on policy and on past performance of the Government. Greg and Frank, along with members of the strategy and policy committee, would gather around the dining room table, each one prepared with two or three questions relating to political information of interest locally and provincially and, in some cases, federally. These questions were placed in a shoe box and I had to draw them out one at a time and give them to Greg, who would read them aloud. I was then given three minutes to present my response. Frank, the timekeeper, would always sit at the head of the table with a stopwatch in his hand. He would vigorously jam in its stem when it seemed that only seconds, not minutes, had passed, so I was always left floundering with the question half-answered when he called time.

The first morning we met, I learned how little I knew about about anything political, and if there had been any way to save face, I would have conceded the election to Dolph right then. When I moaned that the debate would hold me up to public ridicule, that it would be more ignominious for me than a public hanging, Greg said that I was talking nonsense and that all I needed was a little more practice. I stumbled over question after question, taking far too long to get my answer organized, so that Frank always shouted "*Time!*" before I had said anything of substance.

"Cut out the rambling. All that folderol at the beginning," Frank rebuked, time and time again, making scratch-out marks in the air with his ballpoint pen. "Get right to the core of the answer. If they ask you the time, don't feel you have to build them a shaggin' clock. Just give them the time."

I must have looked pretty pathetic during that first session because even Bill Curran said solicitously, "Forget about your blunders now, Tess. That's what we're here for. To get them out of the way. And before we're finished with you, you'll be dreaming politics. You'll know every blunder the Old Man made and, as well, an answer to weasel him out of every one. Just you wait and see."

And Bill was right. I not only dreamt politics, I thought about it twenty-four hours a day. I constantly re-played issues, especially issues pertaining to the Cove. One part of my brain was always reserved exclusively for issues. I could canvass door to door, attend church services, even play bingo, and never for a single moment let my mind be free of trampling over issues.

"Lay your cards on the podium," Frank would tell me over and over again at each morning meeting. He would indicate the handful of 2" x 4" cue cards he had placed on the dining room table. "And when you're answering a question just slip the right card out in front and follow along, point by point like we've laid them out. Like so." He would demonstrate how quickly he could locate the pertinent subject by scanning the block letter heading of each card.

"Let's say you draw a question on increasing the number of hospital beds." He would quickly, almost imperceptibly, rifle through the cards until he came to the one marked HOSPITAL. He would hold it up. "See! 'Tis all here in point form—the number of beds added over the past ten years; the number of patients admitted to the hospital; the projected number of beds that are still needed; the cost per bed."

Once, while on the subject of hospitals, Frank reminded me about the need for an ambulance. For several years now, a hearse has been doing double duty as an ambulance. He warned, "And don't forget you're going to get a question or two about the ambulance. People are fed up with having to go to the hospital in a hearse and some of them think it's up to the government. Can't get it through to them that it's up to the village. But you're not to say right up front that getting an ambulance is up to the village. Agree that 'tis time enough to go in a hearse when you're dead and say you'll try to get the government to kick in."

As the meetings progressed, he would throw the cards aside, saying easily, "Of course you know all this stuff by heart now anyway. But just in case. Besides you can't be expected to keep reams of figures in your head. 'Tis allowed, you know, to have facts and figures jotted down somewhere on cue cards."

I was told again and again that I must not bluff, or, more specifically, I must not be perceived to be bluffing. If I do not know the answer to a question I am to own up to my ignorance in such a way that my ignorance will seem like a virtue.

Greg demonstrated, "Own up that you don't know everything on this particular issue. Say you don't have *all* of the facts and figures on whatever it is you're to discuss. Stress the *all*. Give out what you do have." He looked at Frank for confirmation. "Like Frank keeps saying, don't hee and haw. Leave that to Dolph. Say straight from the shoulder whatever it is you do know. Say it clearly. Firmly. You'd be surprised how few people really listen to the content of any message. It's how you deliver it that counts. And it's how you're perceived. People here are fed up with shysters. Let honesty show through."

Greg made me acquainted with a list of "thou shalt not's" that I must at all times remember. He pressed them home every meeting. "And don't go on and on if you come across a subject you do know. Get right to the meat of it. Give the meat and throw away the fat. Don't be like Dolph. You ask him something and you're always sorry you asked. He goes on and on and on. Just give the facts. Don't waste your three minutes with roundabout stuff. And if you don't know the answer to something, don't let it throw you. Don't let your fluster spoil the questions you do know the answer to."

The cramming of issues into my head, which seems to have been going on for months instead of days, has finally come to an end. This is the day of reckoning. This is the evening of the debate. Greg sent me upstairs two hours ago with a final admonition to rest and relax and then get dressed because I have only a couple of hours before we go to the hall.

But I have only been able to get dressed—the rest and relaxation will have to wait for another time. I have chosen a collarless off-white blouse to soften the severity of my tailored charcoal grey suit. I have settled on a pair of black pumps with heels high enough to give me stature, but low enough to provide comfort. Yesterday I had my hair trimmed so it now falls just short of my collar and it is gleaming jet black from this morning's several rinses in cold water. The mirror tells me that I look intelligent, competent and integrated. My mind tells me I am witless, incompetent and so scattered I'm convinced my body parts are operating independently of my brain. The saliva has disappeared from my mouth and my teeth and tongue seem so oversized I'm certain words will never be able to escape over them or around them. My eyes are scratchy from lack of sleep.

Last night, the more vehemently I told myself to go to sleep, the more vehemently fears and doubts raced through my mind. And not only present fears. Demons from my childhood returned to haunt me and taunt me.

I was once again six years old. I was the Virgin Mary in a Christmas pageant and I had neglected to make a trip to the toilet before going on stage. The mound of hay I was sitting on was getting damper and damper, while off to one side Billy Rowe, dressed in his sister's nightdress and a brownish towel draped over his head, was shouting in an unnatural voice to fellow shepherds: "Let us go over to Bethlehem and see this thing that has come to pass, which the Lord has made known to us."

I was once again seven years old and Sarah Walsh in a fit of jealousy was informing me about my inauspicious beginnings. She was enlightening me on my never-to-be-spoken-about, my never-to-be-seen Yankee father—the father whose war effort consisted of bulldozing a base into existence just outside the Cove and of conceiving me just inside the Cove; the father who was known to me only through a dog-eared photograph. My celluloid sire.

I was once again sixteen years old and suffering the mortification of the damned at the hands of Sr. Clarence. "Tessie Corrigan! Pay attention and stop mooning over Dennis!" Most scalding of all was the fact that Sr. Clarence had used my surname but not Dennis'. Even back then, before my courses in sociology, I was aware of the masses and classes distinction inherent in that omission.

As I tossed and turned and saw night transformed into morning, I visualized worst case scenarios and tortured myself with *what if's*. What if my mind went blank just as I reached the podium? What if I never drew a question I could answer? What if my voice wouldn't carry and the audience had to shout for me to speak louder.

This last "what if" was pure self-flagellation. I have been through several rehearsals or, as Greg called them, "dry runs" at the podium. Over and over again, I have practised speaking from the stage in the church hall, while Greg has listened from a chair at the very back. At the end of my first five minute run-through, Greg said I was so loud and clear that Gabriel wouldn't have needed his horn to hail the good tidings, had I been around at the time.

If I am to survive this debate I must convince myself that today I am the woman in the mirror and not the frightened, insecure child who lurks in my memory.

The hall is packed. Every chair is occupied. People are even standing against the walls and squatting in the aisles. I can view all of this from behind the stage, where I peek out through holes in the tattered curtain. As I did at the beginning of the campaign, I am asking myself how I ever managed to get tangled up in such a situation. I remember how Grandmother used to quote something about a fool returning to his folly like a dog returning to his vomit and I wonder now if I am that fool and if this campaign is my folly. I spent my youth dreaming about leaving the Cove and here I am, more enmeshed in the place than ever before.

There are two podiums and two chairs on the stage. The chairs are for the scrutineers—one to represent each party. The scrutineer's job is to pass the hat to the opposing candidate. After the question has been pulled out, the scrutineer must read it aloud to the audience.

The Master of Ceremonies, who is the president of the Star of the Sea Association, announces that the debate is about to begin and the audience hushes, a few people at a time until there is almost complete silence. By an earlier draw of straws, I am the one to walk on stage first and I do so to a round of applause. Since I have nothing to judge by, I'm not certain whether this hand-clapping can be considered a rousing welcome or whether it is little more than polite acknowledgement of my presence.

Dolph walks across the stage only seconds after I have taken my place at the podium and there is thunderous clapping, much stomping and a few whistles and catcalls. The fact that the hall is top heavy with Tories does nothing to delete last night's *what ifs*. I stand by the podium, clutching it with knuckles as white as death. I feel lightheaded and I realize I'm even forgetting Greg's injunction to breathe through my nose so that oxygen can filter into my lungs. I lay my cue cards—my security blankets—on the podium, reluctant to let them get even this far out of my grasp. My ear drums resound with Frank's final charge: "Give them the issues pure and simple and cut out the shaggin' shit;" and pulsating through my brain is his dire warning that I can either make it or break it for myself in the next four minutes. I picture my parlour ancestors looking down at me, waiting for me to wipe my nose on my sweater cuff or to stammer incoherently.

"Ladies and Gentlemen," I begin, after I have been briefly introduced. "You, the voters in the Cove riding, deserve a representative who has an abundance of energy, a sound educational background, workforce experience and most especially, your interest at heart. You deserve a representative who is honest and forthright and who has dedication and vision. Ladies and Gentlemen, I am that representative."

I receive considerably more applause for this speech than I did when I walked across the stage, and I'm so encouraged by this that my tongue returns to its normal size and the lightheadedness subsides. I am almost eager for the questions to begin.

At the end of the debate, Frank rushes towards me and says that I made the better showing. I beam my thanks even though I know that Dolph's supporters are probably championing him as well. Knots of well-wishers move in to form a thicket around me once I step off the stage. There is much handshaking and many offers of congratulations. Greg flanks my right; Frank my left. Every few moments, Frank squeezes my arm and says in a low but gloating voice, "Shit, girl, you did it. You really did it. The difference was amazing. You could hear a pin drop when you opened with that speech."

Greg's congratulations are more low-key, but he, too, thinks I did well. When Bill Curran tells me it was no fluke that I made a better showing than Dolph, that it was my better preparation that did it, and that I deserve the applause I got, Greg quotes in a mock-sombre tone, " 'Tis not in mortals to command success, but we'll do more Sempronius; we'll deserve it." And I laugh more heartily than the moment calls for, feeling intoxicated in the aftermath of the past gruelling hour.

"What did you do in law school, Greg?" I ask impudently. "Memorize someone or other's Treasury of Quotations? You seem to have a quote to suit every situation."

He jokes that he has a good memory for useless trivia and that he will save his best quotations for my Maiden speech in the House. Frank interjects crustily, "Then, my boy, I suggest you use some of your book-quoting smarts right now on that woman from the paper." He points across the hall to where a woman is sitting on a chair, writing furiously in a note pad propped on her knee.

"You know her?" Frank queries. "Writes for the *Telegram* doesn't she? Get to her before Dolph's henchmen do! Put some of your fancy quotes in there to show her that Tess is a class act." He winks slyly. "Nudge her into writing that Tess has the edge in this campaign. My father always said it don't matter a god-damn what time you get out of bed in the morning as long as you have the reputation of being an early riser." He waves his hands as if to hurry Greg along. "So go on, tout it around that Tess is in the lead and pretty soon she will be."

I'm giddily chiding Frank on his bluffing strategy, telling him you can only bluff some of the people some of the time, when I hear a voice behind me saying, "I'll be along in a minute. I want to say hello to Tessie before I leave."

My words instantly skid to a halt. *Tessie!* No one calls me Tessie anymore. Not even Frank and Rose! I jerk my head around to see who the speaker is and find myself face to face with a stranger—but a *familiar* stranger. I'm so taken off guard that I begin to babble.

"Oh my Lord in heaven! Dennis? Is it you?" I don't wait for an answer, but chatter on, "It is, isn't it?" I notice his Roman collar. "I mean it is you, Father ... Father Walsh? "

Dennis, amused at my embarrassment, gives the impish grin that had always made me hotly defend him to Grandmother whenever she said that Dennis didn't have his own footsteps—just his mother's and they were leading him to Holy Orders. He extends his hand. "Dennis will do the job," he says, still grinning. "That's handle enough."

I extend my own hand, but even in my fluster, when our fingers touch I'm acutely conscious of our flesh against flesh connection. And I'm surprised by the feel of his flesh. I would have expected the hand of a priest to be soft, but Dennis' hand is hard-fleshed. Calloused even. Besides, my memory is of softer hands. Slimmer hands. The hands of an adolescent hesitantly touching my face, fumbling to untie the white plastic collar of my convent uniform. "You pulled off a great evening," Dennis now says, bringing the present back into focus. "I thought you held the crowd spellbound." He says this, even though I know his loyalty is to his brother-in-law, Dolph.

"Evenin' Fadder. Welcome home." Frank politely acknowledges Dennis' presence but quickly and proprietorially cups my shoulder with his left hand, while with his right he uses a paper napkin to mop his face, having long ago given up on his wet cotton handkerchief.

He immediately lets Dennis know that there are two political camps, and that Frank is squarely in mine. "All along we knew she had it in her. We knew she could pull it off. Didn't we, girl?" Even as he speaks, Frank impatiently shifts his weight from one foot to the other. He wants me to be done with Dennis so he can pilot me around the room, working the crowd. This, he told me earlier, will be a time to solidify the votes I presently have and to garner the ones that he believes, to use his own words, "are still up for grabs." He calls these non-committed voters "the nothingarians," and says it is our mandate to convert them. Making small talk with a priest who isn't eligible to vote in the Cove, and who would vote for the oppositon anyway, isn't Frank's idea of time well spent.

Greg, who earlier had stepped aside to speak to a bystander, catches up and it suddenly dawns on me that Greg, who is fairly new to the Cove, may not realize the relationship between Dennis and Dolph. I'm afraid he may say something negative about Dolph's performance. I hurry to introduce Dennis to Greg, making certain the Dolph/Dennis relationship is brought out. The introduction is rushed, fumbled and graceless. Never once in my many fantasy encounters with Dennis did I envision a sweating, flustered Tess floundering for words to stave off a *faux pas*.

Although Greg makes the proper responses, the moment is left awkward and soon everyone begins to move about. Greg excuses himself, saying he wants to see about getting the chairs put back in the storage room. A voter comes up to Frank and involves him in election talk. I'm left alone with Dennis.

"How are you? How is everything?" I ask, groping for words and trying desperately hard to avoid his eyes. I strain to be cool, controlled, collected, but even as I speak I subtly wipe my perspiration-wet hands up and down my thighs. A memory flashes through my mind of the many, many times—although not so many in recent years—I had imagined a chance meeting between Dennis and me. It was always a time, of course, when I would be at my best and he would be filled with regret that he had chosen the priesthood over me. Several years ago I had confessed this fantasy to a close friend and she, in turn, confessed she had similar fantasies about a significant person in her life. She told me that one January day she answered her front doorbell, and there on her steps was the lover of old. At the time, my friend was almost nine months pregnant and she was wearing a pair of her husband's grey woolen socks because slippers wouldn't fit on her swollen feet. Her hair was up in pin curls, every strand plastered to her head in little round circles.

Although my present situation is not as bad as my friend's situation was then, the moment still falls far short of my fantasy and I chatter inanely. "It's been a long time. I hear you're a missionary. El Salvador. That's what Frank says."

Dennis stands before me ramming his hands through his hair, just as I remember him doing whenever he was discomfitted. And, also just as I remember, the sandy-coloured curls drop back down over his forehead, refusing to be controlled.

"Yes, I joined the Missions. The Scarboro Fathers. But not El Salvador. Peru. Just got back last night. For a month."

Because he has now answered all the questions I can think of asking, I'm left to say, "Well, you look great. It must agree with you over there." As I talk, my eyes take in his heavily sun-tanned face and a body build that, like his calloused hands, is not of my memory. My memory also did not programme broad shoulders, deep sun-etched creases around the eyes, and a jawline that has been subjected to daily shaving.

"I don't think I'd recognize you if I met you on the street. Especially with the collar."

He instantly fingers the Roman collar and looks slightly embarrassed. "It's not the place for it, I know. But Sarah was bound and determined that I dress in full regalia." He looks over his shoulder to where Sarah is busily doing what I should be doing, working the crowd.

Dennis' suit looks new and I wonder whether Sarah went to St. John's when she heard he was coming home and ordered the best and the blackest suit that she could find in the stores. And I wonder if she got him home early in the hopes of giving Dolph an even better chance in the election.

But most of all I wonder how Dennis sees me. I'm wishing I had done something different with my hair and regret that my own suit is so severe, so conventional looking. I want Dennis to see me as a sophisticated woman. A woman of substance. A tantalizing mysterious woman—not the impetuous childish Tessie that I am certain is in *his* memory.

As if reading my mind, he says, "You've changed, too. You've changed a lot."

I'm itching to ask him to give me details of the change, but since I only want to be told that the change is for the better, I choose to leave the question unasked. As he did before, Dennis rams his fingers through his hair and smiles his impish smile.

"I came deliberately to see you," he confesses. "Not just on account of Dolph. Although I came for him, too. I couldn't believe it when they told me you were the Liberal candidate, and I had to see with my own eyes."

"Oh ye of little faith," I tease, surprised that I am collecting myself so quickly. "Blessed is he who does not see and still believes."

And even as I'm bantering, I'm managing to think other thoughts—thoughts that have nothing to do with our bumptious encounter. I'm wondering whether it was Sarah who told him about me and, if so, did she also fill him in on my marriage and divorce? And did she tell him that unless my fortunes take a miraculous change tonight, I offer very little opposition to her precious Randolph? And does Dennis realize that I'm well aware of being the dark horse in this election? I don't want him to think that I'm naive enough to believe that I'm a substantial contender for the Cove seat.

I try to finagle the answers to my questions. "You're staying with Sarah, I take it? That's who told you I was Dolph's opposition? And did they tell you that there's about as much chance of the sky falling as there is of my winning this election? That I'm only a shadow opposition?"

"Yes, yes, yes and yes," he answers grinning, adding, "and I'm glad to be home right now because it's a wonderful chance for me to help them out. I can look after the children. With Dolph's campaign, they're on the go a lot." And then, as if forgetting he is speaking with Dolph's opposition, he says, "And Sarah's help will go a long way towards getting Dolph elected. Not that they expect any trouble. But as Dolph says, she's a real asset to him."

I jog his memory that I'm also running in this campaign. "Now that you mention it," I say, my tone mock serious, "that's what I lack. A good wife who would be a real asset. If I had a good wife by my side, Dolph would eat my dust."

Dennis laughs. A "throw-back-the-head" type of laugh. This is a laugh I remember. When he sobers he says, "Well, that's one way you've sure changed. The Tessie I used to know would never concede her opposition had an edge. Even if the edge was a wife."

"I mellowed," I tell him, laughing, suddenly very much at ease with him. "I've mellowed dreadfully. One of the pitfalls of growing up, I guess. Or of growing old. Or whatever."

At this moment Frank, who has never moved far from my side, breaks off his conversation with the voter who had corralled him earlier. He comes over and places his arm around my shoulder, saying hurriedly, "Sorry to have to pull Tess away, Fadder, but I got lots for her to do before the night ends. No rest for the weary."

As I begin to leave, I force myself to say lightly, just as though Dennis were any classmate I had run into after a long absence, "Nice seeing you, Dennis. Maybe I'll see you again before you go back."

"Same here," he responds, equally lightly. He gives me an easy wave of his hand.

I take a couple of steps forward, following Frank, and then I turn my head to give a hasty, backward glance over my shoulder, the way you often do when you part company. Dennis has not moved. He is staring after me. Our eyes meet, and for an instant I'm back in Sr. Clarence's classroom and electrical currents are streaking with lightning speed back and forth between Dennis' desk and mine, sidestepping students on their way to the chalkboard and skirting Sr. Clarence, who is moving in to break the connection before it makes a shambles of her algebra class.

"Come on, Tess. We've wasted too much time already," Frank says irritably, plucking at my elbow, not noticing that a meteor has just spiraled through the roof of the church hall and covered Dennis and me in a shower of sparks. His impatient voice jars me back to a less pleasant present, just as Sr. Clarence's had done when she snapped at me to stop staring at Dennis and pay attention to what she was saying about letting x equal the speed of the train. I give Dennis a small, self-conscious smile and move on.

This morning, in the wake of the debate, electioneering talk has risen to a fevered pitch at the headquarters. Greg is still insisting that issues "pure and simple" will give us the ammunition we need to make an impact in this election and he says he will work unceasingly to hunt down local needs. According to him, a concern for issues coupled with youth involvement will turn the tide for us.

Earlier in the campaign, to entice the youth to our headquarters, he set up a second-hand refrigerator in the back porch and there are always a couple of cases of soft drinks cooling inside it. As well, much to Frank's consternation, Greg installed a stereo in the porch. Frank constantly complains that his nerves are jangled from listening to the *Folsom Prison Blues*. At least once a day he vows to disembowel Johnny Cash. "I swear to God," he threatens, holding his ballpoint pen like a gutting knife, "I'm going to go out there and rip that goddamn Johnny Cash right up the middle. Slit him up the belly like a shaggin' codfish."

This morning, I would eagerly help him silence Johnny Cash's voice—if only I had the energy. My own nerves are in a state of post-debate jangle. Last night I lay in bed, wide awake, minutely going over the debate, holding a post mortem on what I said and what I failed to say, censuring myself for every fumbled question, every wide-of-the-mark answer. And I kept pulling apart that one split second when my eyes met Dennis'. I separated it from other moments, dissected it, searched it for profound meaning, and then castigated myself for making much ado about nothing: Dennis just happened to look my way at the same time I looked his. No more, no less. Yet, try as I might, I could not toss away that one riveting moment.

And the hubbub that has been going on at the headquarters since shortly after seven this morning has only added to my problem. The telephone has been ringing non-stop. We have had an extension put in the pantry and Frank answers all calls, but after he hangs up the receiver he usually shouts out the message to us, whether it is relevant or not. This morning's calls are mostly pleasant ones—complimenting me on last night's performance. But we are also getting a number of issue calls: the road leading to this person or that person's house is a mess; it is a menace for the school bus; the potholes are so big a herd of cattle could disappear into them. Several people called to say that a new snowplough is needed. The old one spends most of the winter in the government garage.

And some of the calls skirt the realm of possibilities for a potential back-benching Member of the House of Assembly. One man has asked what I'm going to do about the Russians because they are destroying the haddock fishery by catching the fish before they spawn. Another voter has registered his protest about lighthouses being automated. He says he'd never trust a machine to know when to blow a fog horn. A third voter wonders whether there is any truth to the rumour that the oil refinery at Come-by-Chance is going to be staffed entirely by Americans. And a fourth says no good will come to me because I broke a chain letter she had sent out.

Frank views all of these calls positively. He says that since they didn't call us in the beginning, they must be starting to think I have a chance of winning and will therefore be in a position to grant them favours. The rest of us don't share Frank's far-fetched faith.

Just a few minutes ago, Frank shouted out that Old Mrs. Benson will vote for me if I can guarantee to have electricity extended to her house—or, as he said, directly quoting Mrs. Benson, if I can guarantee to "give her the lights." Mrs. Benson's house is three miles past the last telephone pole and Frank says she has been making this same request to each party, each election for the past twenty years. He says it's about time Mrs. Benson took the parable of Moses and the Mountain to heart and dragged her little shanty to the nearest telephone pole so she can get it hooked up to the existing power line.

When the phone rings again I say to Greg that this call is probably from someone wanting me to change the direction of the Gulf Stream or give them a government pass to Heaven. However, within a few seconds Frank bobs the receiver in my direction, motioning that it is a personal call. I sense by the way he shuffles the papers around on his desk after he sets the receiver down—in the same hurried way Grandmother used to clear the dishes from the table when she was in a huff—that Frank isn't pleased with this call. My "Hello. Tess speaking," is edged with trepidation.

Dennis' voice is jaunty, buoyant. "Good morning, Tessie. And a beautiful one it is at that."

Although I have harboured the hope that Dennis would telephone, I did not expect him to do so during working hours, and nor did I expect that the call would come so quickly after our meeting. My heart is pounding and my legs are trembling, but still I force myself to sound matter-of-fact.

"Good morning, Dennis. And you're right, it is a beautiful morning." Because I know that Frank and Greg can hear every word I say, my voice comes out of my mouth stilted and thin. I'm wishing I had taken the call in the kitchen and I'm peeved with myself for harbouring guilt when none is deserved. This morning, unlike last night, it doesn't occur to me to call Dennis "Father," and I don't know whether this familiarity has come about because of what he said when I was stumbling over his name when we met, or whether it has

. 104 .

something to do with the intensity of that moment when our eyes locked.

Dennis wants us to have lunch together. "I was just sitting here having my breakfast and thinking it would be a great day for a molasses sandwich at the beach." He rewinds the years. "We could raid your Grandmother's pantry for her freshly baked bread and ..."

I finish his thought. "And we could siphon off some molasses from your Mother's big brown jar. And you could bring your guitar."

"And we'll sing *Hello Young Lovers.*"

"Or *If I were a Backbird.* Although I think I've forgotten the words."

To jog my memory, Dennis begins to sing. "*If I were a blackbird, I'd whistle and sing. I'd follow the ship that my true love sails in. I'd fly to the top mast and there build my nest. And I'd lie like a seagull to his lily-white breast.*"

I nod my head from time to time while Dennis is singing, hoping Frank and Greg will just assume he is talking. Memories tiptoe into my mind: how we used to sneak away each evening after school to our special spot down at the beach—a little sandy alcove between two large boulders that were always so slippery from being covered with wet kelp, we fell over them as often as we climbed over them. We called it our Sheltered Place and we always had to keep an eye out for the tide. On the many occasions when it sneaked in on us we had to scramble up on the boulders to get back on dry land.

"Why can't we meet down there today? For lunch?" Dennis says eagerly. "I'll bring the food. You won't have to worry about a thing." He quickly explains, "Sarah and the children have gone with Dolph for the day and the refrigerator is filled with sandwiches left over from last night. They had a bit of an open house after the debate." I hear him pulling open the refrigerator door so he can list the sandwich types available. "Egg salad. Tuna fish. Cheddar cheese." He chuckles. "But so far no molasses."

"Forget the molasses," I tell him. "I've acquired more exotic tastes—like egg with mayo."

I stretch out the phone cord, forcing it to reach my desk so I can check my schedule. "Oh darn it, Dennis," I lament, running my finger over the day's calendar, "I forgot. I'm already booked." My voice holds such genuine regret that Greg raises his head from his work and gives me a quizzical look. I pointedly ignore him and carry on. "I have a couple of house calls to make shortly after twelve. But tomorrow I'm as free as a bird."

"I have to look after the nephews," Dennis says flatly. The disappointment is now his. "Besides the sandwiches will probably poison us by then." He pauses for an instant as if he, too, is searching for alternatives.

"How about supper?" he asks, tentatively. "I'm free this evening. I'm free then. Same itinerary. Same menu. It will probably be cold down there, but we could dress for it." He pushes the possibility even further. "And I can lay my hands on a bottle of wine and some cheese."

"Now that's an offer I can't refuse." There is a girlish giggle in my voice that vexes me and I try to smother it with humour. "And if you could see my cupboards, you'd understand what I mean. They'd give Mother Hubbard a guilt trip. Even the Third World countries would send me a care package if they could see into my larder."

I hurriedly calculate what time is available to me. Everyone usually leaves the headquarters at four-thirty to give me space to get my supper, although Greg and Frank and I usually come back later. I reason that five-thirty will give me plenty of time to change my clothing and still allow me to be back by seven, in time to put in a couple more hours of work.

"I'll be able to get away around five-thirty. I'll see you then." I end the conversation immediately. When I replace the receiver, the silence is so heavy that I have the feeling I've been talking for hours, although I know it couldn't have been more that two or three minutes.

"I should have used the kitchen phone," I say, by way of apology to Greg and Frank. "Didn't mean to disturb either of you."

"No problem," Greg responds easily, not taking his eyes from the column he is clipping from the newspaper. Frank, however, is not so accommodating.

"Watch out for him," he warns, wagging a finger in the direction of Dolph's house and with not even a hint of humour in his voice. "Collar or not. He's Dolph's brother-in-law. And blood *is* thicker than water. So don't take him into your confidence."

It takes me an instant to process Frank's message. I stare at him dumbfounded. After a second or so, although I'm still flabbergasted, I'm able to ask, "What? What do you mean *'Watch out?'* " All the time I was on the phone, I had imagined Frank thinking licentious thoughts: a man of the cloth, a divorced woman, a clandestine meeting—all the makings of a scandalous tryst. I knew that the minute I ended the call, he would vocalize his thoughts, pointing out that I could not afford to be tainted with a scandal, even an undeserved one. I had my defences prepared for these allegations. I had formed them before I hung up the phone. But now that he is accusing Dennis of seditious intent I find myself at a loss for words.

I stammer, repeating what I've already said, "*What?* What do you mean 'Watch Out!' ... Surely you're not thinking ... Oh, for heaven's sake ... What stupidity. You're being ridiculous." Part of me is relieved that I'm not going to be accused of trysting with a priest, but another part of me is angry at Frank's far-out paranoia. I grab my pencil and begin making heavy-handed deletions in the speech I've been revamping—so heavy-handed that red ink ends up on the page underneath.

When the paper tears, I look over at Greg, a "what next can I expect from Frank" look on my face.

Greg shakes his head and says with mock consternation, "Frank, my son, you're getting more outrageous every day. I think we'll have to put you in a straight jacket before this election is over." He turns to me. "Don't let him get to you, Tess. He's just carrying on to get you going. Even Frank isn't that paranoid."

But Frank lets us know he is indeed that paranoid. He thumps the eraser end of his pencil on his desk like a judge calling order in a courtroom. "Laugh if you will. Yessir. Laugh if you will. Dolph will sabotage you any way he can. Certainly he's been making no bones about calling you a grass widow. And if someone doesn't know what he means by that he comes right out and says your husband is still above the sod even though the marriage has gone under. And he's always referring to you as a divorcee."

Frank mimics Dolph, flattening the "e" on divorcee so that it sounds almost scurrilous. "Tess Corrigan. The divorce-*a* candidate. And you can be sure if you hang around the Holy Father, Dolph'll pump him dry to see what moves you're making."

"Sticks and stones will break my bones," I say sharply, putting Frank in his place because his repetition of Dolph's labels stings painfully. Each time I hear myself referred to as a divorcee, my flesh rips open.

I let Frank know that the old style of politics—a style that could easily be Frank's—doesn't go over anymore. I say, "Surely you realize Dolph isn't endearing himself to the people in the Cove with his name-calling. I've heard he's lost more people than he's gained with his mud-slinging methods."

Greg agrees. "I'm with Tess there Frank. A lot of PC's don't like his way of operating any more than we do. They've told me as much. I think they have their regrets over nominating him."

"Maybe yes, maybe no," Frank hedges. Frank is constantly skirting between Greg's camp and Bill Curran's camp. He now says, "Sometimes I think Bill has the right idea and we should give Dolph as good as he sends. Drop down to his level if we have to." He then remembers that tomorrow I'll be speechmaking at his own house. Rose is hosting a tea for the executive of the Altar Society and both Dolph and I have been invited to give a talk.

"You'll be meeting him close up at Rose's little do tomorrow. Are you ready for that little coming together?"

I glance at my appointment book. "The meeting's at two." I point to the paper before me. "But I'm not sure how ready I am." I again indicate the paper in front of me, with its deletions and insertions and the angry red slash. "That's what I'm doing right now. Revising a speech I gave to the school teachers last week. Rose says most of the women coming have children or grandchildren in high school so it's a good time to really hit hard with the need for more educational opportunities. The need for that technical school."

"That's for sure, girl," Frank easily agrees, his concern over my meeting with Dennis no longer uppermost in his mind. "Lambaste them with the facts. Slap home the facts. And I don't care what anyone says." He looks towards Greg. "If Dolph throws any mud your way, you should throw some back. Like I said, Bill Curran has a point. The only way to shut Dolph's mouth is to fling something in it."

Greg and I have been fighting this battle with Bill Curran since the campaign began. "That's Bill Curran's thinking." I say curtly, letting Frank know that I didn't think he would stoop so low. "I don't happen to go along with Bill's roughshod ways. And I didn't think you did, either."

Frank becomes defensive. "I didn't say I believe in starting the mud-slinging. But I sure as hell don't believe in this other cheek bit either. I'm with Bill there. Sooner or later you have to fight back."

He changes the subject immediately, asking in a bewildered tone, "Why in hell did they nominate Dolph anyway? I can't figure that one out. They have plenty of good people in their camp. People anyone could respect no matter what his politics."

Greg supplies a reason. "I think it has something to do with the times. Everything is youth oriented. Dolph can't be much more than thirty-five or thirty-six. And Tess being young. They wanted someone to offset her."

Frank slaps his desk and laughs, flitting to another subject. "Youth! Now that's a subject you should hear our Bill get going on. He really goes wild about those hostels that are springing up everywhere. Supported by the government. Hotels for layabouts, he calls them. Says our poor fishermen are flying in rags, while the young people are flying in airplanes. Landing in St. John's from the Mainland in droves and getting next-to-free lodgings."

I glance into the pantry at Bill's empty desk. "By the way," I say, "speaking of the devil, where is Bill? He's usually the first one in."

Frank also looks at Bill's desk. "Oh I forgot, I guess. I meant to tell you Bill went to Corner Brook for some sort of meeting about garages."

"Isn't that Dolph's old stomping ground? Isn't that where he had his business before he came here?" asks Greg.

"I believe 'tis," Frank says. "I think he had a business in Corner Brook. Although I believe he came from away originally. Sydney, I think. Or maybe he went to Sydney and then came back." Frank gives a biographical sketch of Dolph. "His parents or his grandparents, I don't know which, were from the West Coast. I'm not sure whether they moved away or what."

The ringing of the telephone halts our conversation. Frank reaches for the receiver and with his hand resting on it, he offers me one last cautionary word. "About getting chummy with Dennis, girl, I don't mean to be preachy, but you should give the Holy Father a wide berth until after the election." Just before he picks up the receiver he adds, in a tone that tells me he knows the folly of giving me good advice, "But 'tis like my poor mother always said, have it your own way and the devil will have you that much sooner."

Greg and I exchange "here we go again" looks and then burst out laughing. Frank uses his mother for all dire sayings. We both return to the work at hand—I to the speech and Greg to perusing the newspapers for political news. Greg clips out all the pertinent information he believes I should know and I have to read it before I go to bed. He maintains that while the House is in Session and each day's papers are filled with special releases, it is imperative that I be acquainted with what is being reported. As well, I must keep up federally. He is adamant that I must not be perceived to be ignorant of Canadian politics—locally, provincially or federally.

I force myself to concentrate on renovating my speech, but because of Dennis' call, the interest is gone. I look at my watch. I count the hours until five-thirty. I begin to worry that something will come up and we will have to stay after the usual closing time. I mentally go through my wardrobe, wondering what I have brought out from St. John's that will be suitable for an evening in late May, on a beach where the inshore wind can be cold even on the hottest day in August. Settling on nothing, I force myself to go back to revamping my speech so that I will be able to make my house calls on time.

All the while I'm making the house calls, my mind is on my meeting with Dennis. When I notice I'm taking longer than I intended, I begin to fret that Dennis will come to the house and I won't be there to meet him. When I finally do get back to headquarters, Greg and Frank have already gone—as I had hoped—and on the kitchen table, left out for my viewing, is a clipping from the morning paper about last night's debate. The instant I notice it, I reach to pick it up and then draw back as though someone has jabbed me with a pin.

"Don't touch that! It'll just spoil your evening with Dennis," I reprimand myself sternly, even as I'm reaching out to pick it up. With much apprehension I begin to read it.

LOCAL CANDIDATES PERFORM

Last night the people in the Cove riding were given a clear insight into the qualifications of the two candidates representing them in the upcoming by-election. Promises, promises and promises fell faster than the leaves from an aging tree during a northeast gale. Randolph Simmons, PC candidate, spoke about the poor performance of the present government. He also spoke about the importance of jobs, better roads and the need for an ambulance to service the Cove area. If he is elected he will search out more jobs for the unemployed in the Cove and he will work towards improving the condition of the roads. He gave assurances that one of his major priorities would be obtaining government money for an ambulance. He also said that he sees the need for a new deck on the bridge that joins the Cove South and Cove North.

Tess Corrigan, Liberal candidate, and the first woman to offer in a Newfoundland election, gave the government credit on a number of issues, including increased spending on education, the establishment of a timberboard mill on the West Coast and the Come-by-Chance oil refinery. She emphasized that if she is elected, she will dedicate her efforts to helping the youth of the Cove, particularly the youth who want to take post-secondary education. She gave particular attention to the youth drain from the community and said she will do everything possible to see to it that a school of technology is located in the area. She will also direct her efforts towards putting an extension on the old age home—an infirmary addition—so that the people in the Cove won't have to leave the home when they get ill. She said that while she sees the need for an ambulance, she couldn't offer much concrete hope in this area because it is the responsibility of the Village Council to obtain such a service, but that she would do all she could to seek government assistance towards the purchase of such a vehicle. She said she offers her constituents energy, honesty, integrity, dedication and vision.

It would appear, from the applause when the candidates came forth separately after the question and answer period, that Tess Corrigan had edged out in front of Randolph Simmons. However, since the Cove is a Progressive Conservative bastion, a victory in this debate does not necessarily signal a victory at the polls.

I read the clipping again and again, especially the last paragraph. My credibility is spread out before me in print and I relish each word. I wonder what Frank and Greg said to each other when they read it. I'm sure Frank, the eternal political optimist, scoffed at the last line. Logic and reason are not Frank's strong suits during election times.

I look at my watch and I see that I have really let the time get away from me. "Oh Good Lord," I say, in a voice that is almost a shriek. "Dennis will be here in a half hour and I won't be ready."

I decide there isn't time to wash my hair but then decide I must wash it even if I don't have time to dry it. It is saturated with smoke. Bedridden Mrs. Whalen, with whom I spent most of the afternoon, smoked so heavily that when her son came into the room he quipped that he would soon have to install a foghorn in order to navigate his way to her bed.

I dash up to my bedroom to get ready, leaving the

hall door open so I can hear the telephone if it rings. I rapidly scan my closet and settle on a green cardigan and pleated wool skirt, deciding this is just the outfit to stave off the cold wind. But as soon as I'm dressed, I take the outfit off and reach for my jeans and off-white fisherman-knit pullover. The jeans haven't been worn for several weeks and I have to crowd myself into them, lamenting the good hospitality of the Cove voters—and the pound here from homemade jam, the pound there from buttermilk biscuits. I am more frenzied than I was just minutes before going on the stage for the debate, and I know if Frank were to see me like this he would chidingly mention that this is not suitable behaviour for a potential Member of the House.

While I'm still in the process of brushing my hair, hair that hasn't had time to fully dry, I'm startled by Dennis' voice shouting from the kitchen.

"Hello. I'm here. I'll just make myself at home." His voice filters up to my bedroom from the open hall door.

Having lived in the downtown section of Montreal, where I had every door and window double-barred, I'm still having difficulty getting used to the Cove custom of not locking doors and of visitors simply walking in without knocking.

I shout back to Dennis that I'll be down in a minute and immediately throw the hairbrush aside, reconciling myself to letting the wind do the rest of the arranging and rearranging of my hair. I take one last glance in the mirror over my bureau before racing down over the stairs.

Dennis is standing by the window looking out at the overgrown meadows. Because I'm wearing soft-soled shoes, he doesn't hear me come in and I have a second to appraise him before he turns around. Like me, he is wearing a fisherman-knit sweater and jeans. In the secular clothing, I can see a stronger resemblance than I did last night to the young man Grandmother always called "Eileen's Dennis."

Sensing my presence, he suddenly turns to face me. He gives me a diffident smile, like me, uncertain how to begin this meeting. He hesitates a moment and then extends his hand. "Hi! Hope I'm not too early."

All the while I was dressing I wondered whether I should shake hands with him as I would do with a stranger or near stranger, or whether I should ignore such formality and get on with the conversation just as if I were greeting Greg or Frank. Or, indeed, whether I should hug him, as was our custom upon meeting and leaving. Dennis' outstretched hand makes the decision for me. His handshake is stronger than last night's. I feel the heat of his fingers pressing against my own. And the handshake is longer than last night's. After the greeting, neither of us makes any attempt to disjoin our hands and we stand in the middle of the kitchen, hands clasped at arm's length. I suddenly become shy and adolescent. I try to smile, but my lips barely part. The moment floats in the air, discomposed. It drifts from the present to the past and back again. Then, as if on cue, our joined hands break away and awkwardly drop by our sides. Each of us moves back a pace and we begin talking at the same time, our voices louder than necessary, as if we need loudness to centre us in the present.

"We'd better be going," we say in unison and then laugh at our clumsy attempt to be nonchalant. The tension breaks.

"I feel like a school kid," Dennis confesses, fidgeting with the back pack of sandwiches he has strapped on his shoulders. He gives a self-deprecating laugh. "I'm usually extremely *suave* and *debonair*. Not this clumsy."

I confess I had pondered over the protocol of our meeting. "While I was getting dressed, I wondered whether we should shake hands, give a friendly hug, or just say hello, with you staying on one side of the braided rug and me on the other."

Dennis laughs again and then dashes any hope

I may have harboured that he only remembers the finer qualities of my adolescent self. He says, his eyes twinkling, "The Tessie I used to know wouldn't have spared too many minutes on such concerns. She would have done what she felt like doing, and like your grandmother used to say, let the devil take the hindmost."

I laugh, remembering. "She used to say that all the time. 'Tessie Corrigan, you're so headstrong that no matter what I say, you go right ahead and do what you want to do anyway and let the devil take the hindmost.' " I want to let Dennis know that light years separate the Tessie he remembers and the Tess I have become, but all I say is that we had better get going or the sandwiches will spoil and we'll both end up with salmonella poisoning.

"Now wouldn't that be an Alfred Hitchcock twist," Dennis laughs. "Can't you see the headlines: 'Liberal Candidate Poisoned by Tory Sandwiches.' "

I tell him that Frank wouldn't see the slightest bit of humour in that remark and that his paranoia is beginning to verge on the totally irrational. "You realize, of course, that if Frank had his way he'd bring in a dog to sample the sandwiches before I'd be allowed to let them pass my lips." I recount Frank's earlier conversation. "And he was really serious about the dangers of fraternizing with you."

Dennis chuckles. "I can hear him now. Same old Frank. He'd probably frisk the Pope if he came directly from Dolph's place to here."

I make a quick check around the kitchen to see that the ashtrays have been dumped and that there is nothing left near the stove to catch on fire and then we leave for the beach, each of us wondering out loud whether the short-cut over the cliff has become overgrown to such an extent that we will have to forego it and take the long way around.

The path is indeed overgrown, but we attempt it anyway. The short-cut begins in the pasture behind my house and ends with a five-foot drop over a sheer-faced rock to the beach below. It is a tangle of alder bushes and scrub spruce. Dennis pilots the route, and like Moses parting the Red Sea, he parts the canopied branches, some of which are so supple they snap back as though their limbs are connected to their trunks with spring hinges.

From time to time, when some sapling whisks past his waist, Dennis shouts a warning, delivering me from imminent decapitation. "Watch out! Some of these are like slingshots."

He also calls my attention to stumps and rocks underfoot, but because I am following so close to him, most of the time I am already stumbling by the time I get his warning. We laugh as I go reeling towards one side of the path or the other, and sometimes I have to clutch at his waist for support. Sometimes he reaches behind himself to steady me, his hands a gentle pressure on my sweatered arm. Even though the touching is only momentary, warmth spreads over my body and lasts long after the contact is broken.

At the end of the path Dennis unharnesses his backpack, lowers it down to the beach and leaps after it. He then pushes the backpack out of the way and reaches up to clasp both of my hands. I jump outward, landing in the sand, facing him. We are only inches apart. Just as they did last night after the debate, our eyes meet and again they hold. This time, though, as if our actions have been choreographed, we quickly break the contact and each of us takes a step backwards. To further distance ourselves from each other, we fidget. Dennis rams his hands in his pockets and I tug at the cuffs of my sweater sleeves, pulling them down over my hands as though it has become imperative that every piece of exposed flesh be covered. I notice the muscles in Dennis' neck tightening and I know the moment is as tension-filled for him as it is for me. I frantically search for something to say, erratically discarding sentence after sentence and not giving voice to any of the thoughts that are surging through my mind.

Just when it seems we are not able to move beyond this emotional moment, Dennis stoops down, retrieves the backpack and hoists it to his shoulders. "That's it over there isn't it? That's the spot," he asks, even though he already knows the answer. He nods toward a large rock a few feet away and covered with wet green kelp, and begins walking towards it. The intimacy instantly shatters and we both make believe the moment never happened.

Once we climb the rock and settle our stuff down on the lee side of it, I set up the picnic, opening the cellophaned sandwiches. Dennis uncaps the wine. He hunkers down in the tide-wet sand and pours a small amount of wine into a styrofoam cup, tastes it and grimaces.

"Yuck!" he says, wiping his mouth with his hand. "I'm no connoisseur of wine, but this must be the cheapest of the cheap." He points to the "made in Canada" label. "Rot-gut my Father would call it. Talk about as bitter as gall."

I drop down beside him and hold my cup out to him for a fill-up so I can make my own assessment. I take a mouthful, swallow it and make the same grimacing face that Dennis made.

"At least no one can accuse the Tories of overspending on booze," I say, scrupulously straight-faced. "This stuff tastes like embalming fluid. Not that I've ever tasted embalming fluid."

Dennis throws back his head and laughs. Then he

straightens up, becomes serious and takes another sip, this time letting the liquid slowly swirl around in his mouth as though he is a knowledgeable wine-taster.

"No. Not embalming fluid," he says, speaking gravely. "But perhaps essence of vinegar. No feet ever trampled over fine grapes for this brew."

I scrunch the bottom of my cup into the sand so it will stand upright, and reach for a sandwich. After I take a bite, I pause in my chewing. "You know something Dennis," I say, in the same earnest tone he had used, and pointing to the wine bottle that is propped beside the rock. "This would be a good time for you to test your mettle. And it's not like you'd have to start from scratch. Like from plain water or anything. All we'd need here is a switch from domestic to imported." I purse my lips, thinking of acceptable wines. "You know, nothing exotic. *Blue Nun* would do. Or *Black Tower*." I flutter my hand from one side to the other. "Just something in the medium range. Not too high. Not too low."

Dennis and I were always able to finish each other's thoughts and it is obvious we still have the ability to do this because now he furrows his brow as though he is pondering both the obstacles inherent in upgrading this cheap domestic wine and his ability to replicate the miracle of the Wedding Feast of Cana.

After a few ponderous seconds, he asserts. "Far too complicated, Tessie." His tone leaves no room for contradiction. "It's out of the question. Completely out of the question."

He continues in a mock-serious voice. "Not that I couldn't pull it off. I could do it just like that." He snaps his fingers. "Zap! *Blue Nun*. Zap! *Black Tower*." He shrugs, pursing his lips, "A little something from the Tuscany Valley, maybe? You name it and with a flick of the wrist, I could set it before you." He then explains why he chooses to renege on the miracle.

"Too much bureaucracy. I'd be accused of dodging

provincial sales tax. The unions would jump all over me because I don't pay into the Local. And to boot, I don't have my distiller's certificate. So they'd be sure to get me on that."

"Well not to worry," I say airly, reaching for my cup and washing my sandwich down with the bitter wine. "At least we can take consolation in the fact that this stuff will kill any bacteria that might be hovering around in the sandwiches. Certainly if I were a bacterium, I'd rather commit hari-kari than hang around in this stuff."

I toss my empty cup in the direction of Dennis' backpack, to be picked up later and taken home with us. Then I change the subject abruptly, "But enough about the wine, Dennis. I want to hear about you."

"Such as?" he inquires, squinting his eyebrows into a question mark.

"Such as everything since I last saw you."

He chortles, making my request sound out-rageous. "*Everything*? For the past twelve years? Whew! That's asking a lot. Would you settle for a paraphrased and summarized account?"

"Well, as Sr. Clarence always said, if you can't get what you want, you learn to want what you get." I jog his memory. "And, by the way, it's closer to thirteen years. But who's counting?"

Dennis adjusts his position in the sand, stretches his legs out and leans his back against the large boulder that is sheltering us. He carefully looks for a spot that isn't covered with wet kelp, but finding none, leans back anyway.

"Went to University of Toronto for two years. On to St. Augustine's seminary in Scarborough. Ordained especially for the Scarboro Foreign Missions. Mother and Father on hand for my ordination and first mass. Off to Peru. Various missions there. Mountain villages mostly. Home for a month or so for rejuvenation and then ..."

He breaks off, shakes his head as if the future is a

question mark. "And then who knows?" He waves his hands in a submissive gesture. "These are troubled times for missionaries, but I'll go where I'm sent."

His biographical data isn't specific enough to satisfy my penchant for detail, so I dig for more information.

"And what exactly do you do there? In Peru? Proselytize?"

"A little. In the Third World countries the Scarboro Fathers' concept of Church and Gospel has just as much to do with feeding the body as it has to do with feeding the soul."

He looks out to sea—out beyond the waves that hug the shore, out to where the water flattens and settles down. "And God knows there's enough to do along those lines. There's always a crop failure, a drought, a hurricane, a revolution, a roof blowing off, and more sickness than we ever heard of." He adds, and his voice is very solemn, "I do whatever needs to be done."

He shifts his position against the rock and with it his mood, reminding me that he is back home to get a reprieve from sad pictures. He chuckles and says, "Remember when you used to snark at me that I was hell bent on becoming Marrying and Burying Sam and that nothing you could say or do would make a difference to me? And remember how you used to accuse me of wanting my own confessional—a sin box, you called it—so I could feel good hearing about how bad others were."

I reach out to capture a piece of rogue cellophane that is trying to escape in the wind. "Don't remind me!" I say, shamefaced. "What an insufferable brat I was."

He smiles, a faraway smile. "That you were," he agrees. "But back then I was pretty insufferable myself. I was more pious than the Church."

"And that you were," I parrot. "Tell me about it." My tone is playfully sardonic. "The way you used to talk I was sure that by now you'd be giving me your blessing from the Vatican balcony."

I look at him and my look asks, where did all of his lofty plans go? I smile impishly. "How come you haven't even made Cardinal yet! The least I expected was a red biretta."

Dennis' voice holds a mischievous smile. "So I bragged a lot back then. So you mouthed off a lot. If I remember correctly, you were going to be a reporter for the *New York Times*."

"Come off it, Dennis," I scold, although only the words are scolding. "Don't make me appear worse than I was. It was the *Daily News* I intended to work on. That was as far as my aspirations went. I didn't even know the *New York Times* existed. All I wanted was out of the Cove. Far away." I giggle. "And I thought St. John's was far away."

I turn the conversation back to his life. "Let's not get side-tracked here. I want to know what made you change your sights from being His Holiness?"

He reaches in front of him and scoops up a handful of sand and lets it trickle out of his fingers. All roguery dissappears. "Sharing, not accumulation. Service, not power," he says soberly as though he is repeating a mantra, and as though the phrases should be meaningful to me. He hauls his knees up toward his chin and places his elbows on them, hands together, fingers steepled.

He speaks quietly. "Took on a different focus, I guess. And certainly missionary work is not the way to network yourself into the Vatican." He shrugs and his mood lightens. "But I tossed aside that ambition long ago. And just as well, probably."

As he is talking, I dig deep in the sand and absently watch the hole fill up with water. After a minute or so I hold up my hands, fingers wide apart, to let the tiny grains of sand fly away in the wind. I watch them disappear like a flock of wild ducks heading out to sea.

Without taking my eyes from the vanishing sand, I blurt out, surprising even myself. "Are you happy with your choices Dennis? Are you happy with yourself?" Embarrassed at being so direct, I hurry to amend, "I don't mean to take your psyche apart or anything, but you always seemed to know what you wanted and I just wondered if everything turned out well."

He ponders for a moment before replying. He unsteeples his fingers and steeples them again. "Well ... Gosh ... I don't know how to answer that." He shifts his weight against the rock and rubs his shoulder blade where the dampness has penetrated his wool sweater. "Contented. Maybe. Although sometimes I'm not so sure that's the appropriate word."

Again he turns and looks out toward the ocean, but this time he focuses closer to shore at a wave that is pulling away from the beach and growling like a hungry dog being hauled away from its supper. The wave recedes despite its protests, and Dennis' eyes follow it out to the spot where it gathers force to lash in on the shore again.

"Sometimes I'm convinced I make no more of an impact over there than that gull feather that was pulled out with that wave." Once again he turns sombre, and as he talks his voice is so soft it seems he is talking more to himself than to me. He looks directly at me and his eyes are filled with uncertainty. "Tessie, sometimes I wonder what I'm doing over there. All of your efforts seem so futile sometimes. You get so discouraged. You come away wondering if you made any difference at all."

He shrugs and his mood becomes more upbeat. "But I guess I'm no different from others who've gone my way. We find it hard to accept a world that lacks social justice." He shrugs again, and not wanting to set priests apart from others, adds, "For that matter, who amongst us doesn't yearn for peace and reconciliation amongst all people?" He rubs his eyes, gouging them roughly with his knuckles, seeming to shut out pictures of man's inhumanity to man. "But over there we see so much disparity. You've no idea. So much need. You can't just walk away from it." He sighs heavily and again looks out to sea.

As always, I envy Dennis his spiritual passion, his relentless dedication. In earlier days I would have made a smart remark, aiming to make light of his dogged earnestness, although I would have given anything to have had this steadfast passion myself. Now I simply inquire whether he has ever considered opting for a less stressful way of carrying out his vocation.

"Have you considered parish work back here? In Canada? If it's need you're looking for, you can find plenty of it on this continent."

He agrees easily. "Oh there's need alright. No doubt about that. But it's a case of degree of need."

Remembering what he said about my taunts regarding a confession box, I quip. "And I still think you'd be just right for that confession box." With my fingers, I mischievously write his name in the air as though I were writing it over a confessional. "Fr. D. Walsh—Marrying and Burying and Unburdening." I give him a lightly appraising look, taking in his boyish handsomeness. "On the other hand," I say scampishly, "maybe I should write Father What-a-Waste. You know, like the convent girls used to call any priest who didn't happen to look like the old fellow on the cover of that almanac that used to come in the mail every fall. Dr. Chase I think his name was. Had a long beard. Advertised cure-all ointments."

Dennis flicks a pinch of sand in my direction. His face lights up with a grin. "Same old irreverent Tessie. Good thing for you God knows you pretty well. And knows it's all a front. I don't think He'd put up with you otherwise."

He reaches for a tuna sandwich, breaks off a corner and throws it to a seagull that for the last several minutes has been taking jerky hesitant steps in our direction. When Dennis throws out the food, the gull nervously flutters backwards, then quickly recovers its courage and comes close enough to swipe the bread and swallow it in one laborious gulp, ready for a second handout. Dennis obliges, tossing out another corner of sandwich before returning to my question.

He admits, sighing as if he is embarrassed by the temptation, "Yes, I'm sorry to say there've been times when I've been tempted to have that little church in the wildwood. Severely tempted. Especially when Mother and Father were alive. But I'm much too selfish for that sort of life, Tessie. Far too selfish."

His sincerity is so whole-souled that I feel a catch in my throat. I don't even question his statement, which to me holds so much contradiction. In his place, I would have used "selfless."

He gives me a direct look, a forthright look, and his eyes are the eyes of the young Dennis—the Dennis who was certain he could make a difference.

"Would you think of me as selfish, Tessie, if I told you I like the serenity I get from helping the destitute? And that I relish the peace I get from living amongst peasants."

I arch my eyebrows, not quite understanding. Living in a primitive village has never been my idea of decadence and my mind is thinking sacrifice rather than selfishness.

He elaborates. "These people speak with such simplicity. Similar to the Gospel. They often speak more profoundly than the most articulate theologian. And their words are always so simply put. Being amongst them keeps me in touch. Keeps me centred."

I look down at the ground, humbled in the presence of such lowly aspirations. Dennis suddenly changes the subject, as if he has caught himself going on too long about his own life. "But enough about me. What about Tessie Corrigan?"

I've never felt that my life could stand up to scrutiny—and I especially feel this way now, after hearing Dennis' account of his life. I toss my hands in the air cavalierly, signifying that my life is, and has been, miniscule. I have not weathered a flood, a drought, or a revolution. Nor have I converted pagans. I haven't even forgiven Leonard for committing adultery with his paralegal.

"Paraphrased, summarized and encapsulated it goes like so," I say hurriedly, ashamed of my small existence. "Entered convent. Left convent. Worked in travel agency in Montreal. Worked. Worked. Worked. Studied. Studied. Studied. Married Leonard. Unmarried Leonard. Manager of travel agency in St. John's. And the folly of my life—candidate for the Cove. Over and out."

Dennis stretches his legs, dumps the sand out of his shoes and again rubs his shoulder where the damp, kelpy rock has been pressing against it. He is silent for so long I'm wondering whether he heard anything I said or whether he tuned out my recounting early on because of its lack of substance.

"So!" I say, prompting a response, fretting that he isn't asking for more detail. Even small lives can be spiced up with minutiae, and I could easily enlarge upon mine if he were to show any interest.

When he finally speaks, what he says takes me by surprise. "And *you*, Tessie? Are *you* happy?" He asks this with such concern, I find it impossible not to respond, even though I have always steered clear of examining my life in terms of happiness or unhappiness. I have always avoided it as though it were an undertow capable of sucking me into deep, dark water.

"Turn about is fair play," he prods, teasing, sensing this question is one I would rather ask than answer.

Because I really want to give him an answer, I hurriedly run through the status quo of my present existence, tramping through its hills and valleys, but I'm no closer to finding an answer when I finish than when I started.

"As God is my judge, Dennis," I say truthfully, "I really don't know whether I'm happy or unhappy. Or none of the above." I laugh lightly, hoping a frivolous reply will satisfy him. "Sometimes I think I'm just terminally maladjusted."

Dennis laughs, too, but then says seriously, "Don't cop out on me by getting glib, Tessie."

"I'm not copping out," I tell him truthfully. "It's just that I really don't know if I'm happy or not. And contrary to what Socrates said, the unexamined life is worth living."

He laughs again and reaches over, lightly touching my shoulder. "You sound just like one of my superiors, Monsignor Whalen. He used to say that if you have to keep asking yourself if you're happy with your vocation, then the answer is no. So maybe you're deliriously happy and don't know it."

I shake my head. "Naw, that's not true. On a scale of one to ten, I'm about a six." I don't tell him that I have surmised for some time that I harbour an entrenched melancholy deep inside me. "I'm too much of a worrier to be deliriously happy. I'm always worrying about something. About everything. Mostly about tomorrow. The future. And even when I have nothing special to worry about, I dredge up something, just to keep the gods appeased." I jokingly tell him about my feeling that if the gods get the notion I'm too happy they'll become jealous and send me a boxcar full of troubles.

When he asks for examples of the things I worry about, I dig into my storage bin and pull anxieties out at random. I pull them out in the full realization that I'm too young for some of them and too old for some of them and that Dennis will probably ridicule me for all of them. But I give them to him anyway.

"Being lonely. That's one," I say. "I'm terrified of one day becoming so severely lonely that I'll take to peeking around my curtains at the mailman, hoping he'll turn up my driveway, even if it is only to bring me junk mail."

I recount my meeting with a woman whom I had met through a want ad in the classified section of the *Montreal Gazette*. She was selling off her household belongings piecemeal, in dribs and drabs, through classified ads. When I asked her why she hadn't sold it all at once, explaining she would have saved money on the advertisement, she had said she wanted visitors, and she wanted to stretch out people coming to her house as long as possible, even if they were only coming to cart away a rug, a dish or a battered bureau.

When Dennis nods and says, "Yes, I'd say that's being severely lonely alright," I again dig into the storage bin. "And I worry about getting old. I worry about face wrinkles and neck folds and dimples in my elbows and whether any man will love me when I have to sally forth in a flowered fat dress."

"I'll still love you, Tessie. I'll always love you, no matter what," Dennis says, all traces of humour suddenly disappearing from his voice.

I'm so startled by the change in his tone that I dart him a direct look and I see such sincerity in his eyes, that tears begin to smart in the corners of my own. And I know he speaks the truth. Dennis had continued to love me even when I wasn't very lovable. He had loved me through my rages over the man who had married my mother and conceived me even though he had a wife and children back in the States. And he had loved me through the stormy times when I was angry at

Grandmother because she was attempting to tame my tempestuous nature. He had even loved me during the many times I had called God to task for letting Martin, my surrogate father, die. And because I'm afraid that the tender feelings in my heart are now mirrored on my face, I look away from him and say blithely, "And tell me, Father Dennis, will I get all of this unconditional love without having to be a peasant or a pagan, or a Peruvian farmer with a crop failure."

"Certainly," he says, catching my mood. "You could even be an Infidel, and I'd still love you. Or a Heretic. Or for that matter," he says, referring to my old second-hand two-door Corvair, that happens to be red, "you could even be so materialistic you'd drive a flaming red sports car."

"And what if I told you that I worry about going to heaven? All that sitting around. Eternal confinement. Nowhere to go on weekends. Same faces day after day."

Dennis pulls back in mock horror. "Well, I do have my limits. I'm not a fountain of love, or anything."

We both laugh at our silliness. Suddenly I realize I'm ravenously hungry. "Now, speaking of far out worries," I joke, "would you toss me one of those sandwiches that Frank thinks are instruments of Tory sabotage."

Dennis passes the sandwich container and pours what is left of the wine into my cup. I pull the bread apart. "You don't suppose Frank could be right and Dolph put a little dollop of botulism in here?"

"Well, come to think of it," Dennis says, mischief in his voice, "I haven't seen the old gull that ate my handout come back again. He's probably sprawled out somewhere with *rigor mortis* setting in." He picks up a sandwich and bites into it, and in a few seconds directs the conversation back to my life.

"Would it be prying too much if I asked you about

your marriage? You know, about the break-up? Sarah told me it didn't last long."

"Oh yes, the little matter of the break-up," I say saucily, the wine making my tongue far too nimble. I squirm around, making believe I am settling in for a long siege and that he had better make himself comfortable too. I drop my voice, in keeping with the solemnity of the tale to come. "Chapter One," I say gravely and somberly. "It was a dark and stormy night ..."

"Tessie!" Dennis' voice holds a gentle reprimand. "You're doing it still. Being flip. Like you always did when you were hurting. Pretending it doesn't matter."

Chastened, I pull my face into a small smile. "Yeah, you're right, Dennis. I am being flip. Sometimes it helps you know. But then sometimes it doesn't."

I shuffle myself into seriousness and prepare to give him the unvarnished truth. "The fact is, there's very little to say about my marriage. Leonard and I careened toward each other, both of us rebounding from an emotional crisis. Leonard's soon-to-be bride had up and left him for someone else, practically at the altar, and I had just buried the last of the Corrigans—other than myself, of course—and was wondering who was going to be on hand to plant me in the ground when my time comes. Or who would wipe the drool from my face after my stroke." I wave my hands to take in all the horrific possibilities that await the alone and the lonely. "Or who would pretend I'm not talking nonsense when I insist that the electric organ in my living room transmits everything I say to the Mounties." I shrug, knowing I haven't the words to convey to him why it had seemed so right at the time for Leonard and me to marry. So I say limply, "So there we were, two shaken people and well ... well ... we simply merged our fears and our hurts, hoping it would be better to bear and share together."

I again gesture with my hands, this time dismissively, as if to say "that's the sum and substance of my story." But now it is Dennis who wants details.

"That's how you got married. Will you tell me how you got unmarried?"

I give a short, sardonic laugh. "That's easy enough to tell. Leonard's fly-away ladybird flew back home. On American Airlines. Economy fare. Los Angeles. Chicago. Toronto. Practically landed in Leonard's arms. And practically before the ink was dry on our marriage licence."

I chant softly, although I'm not sure why, "*Ladybird, Ladybird, fly away home. Your house is on fire, your children will burn.*"

I break off chanting and continue my recounting. "It seems Ladybird had second thoughts about a lifetime of surfing with a drop-out graduate student from the University of Toronto. Things like three square meals a day began to take on new meaning and Leonard's stability started to look pretty good to her."

I give another little laugh, a too-hard laugh. This is not the picture of myself I want to leave with Dennis. "I heard she flew off because she hated the way Leonard skimmed his spoon across the cream in his coffee cup, as though he were removing congealed fat from a pan of gravy. At least that's what she told Leonard's mother. And his neatness almost drove her wacko. Especially the way he placed his shoes in the closet—toes in, heels out. But I guess when you're caught in traffic on a Los Angeles highway and the landlord is hounding you for rent, these things don't seem so important."

To improve my image in Dennis' eyes, I'm wishing I could refer to this woman who replaced me in Leonard's affections as "Monica," but even after all of the time that has passed, I still find it hard to dignify her with a name. Dennis is now left to refer to her as "Ladybird."

"How did you find out about Ladybird? Did Leonard confess?" Dennis surprises me with this question because it is one I usually only get from other women who themselves have been deceived. The fashion in which the disclosure is made doesn't appear to be as important to men.

"No, Leonard didn't tell me. *She* was the one who told me. I hadn't an inkling anything was going on." I shake my head, recalling how unprepared I had been for Monica's news. "Not an inkling. I didn't even know she was back home so I never gave it a second thought when Leonard started going to Toronto on trumped-up business trips."

Little tremors of pain, of the same genre, but down-scaled from the ones I had felt when the affair first went public, flutter in my stomach. "I found out about the liaison from a phone call. From *her*. About three months into the affair. And a couple of days before Christmas. I guess she was afraid Leonard wouldn't have the courage to tell me—he was never big on facing unpleasant situations—and she didn't want to continue in the role of backstreet wife. Or maybe she got roiled up because I had a free trip to Hawaii through Sperry Travel—highest number of sales for the year—and Leonard was included in the freebie." I shrug my shoulders and arch my eyebrows in a who-knows-why gesture. "Or maybe it was because she couldn't bear the thought of me filling Leonard's Argyle Christmas sock."

I swipe at my face with my sweater sleeve, not sure whether I'm wiping away tears or the spray from the waves that are creeping higher and higher.

Dennis reaches out and pulls me to him, enclosing me in warmth, and I feel as secure as I used to feel whenever Grandmother would tuck an extra wool quilt around me on stormy nights as we sat in front of the fire. "Puffs" she used to call the patchwork quilts; but Martin called them "ballast for the Queen Mary."

Dennis' compassion unleashes emotions in me that I had packed away in Montreal—packed away in tightly sealed cartons along with my Christmas decorations, fully intending to open them up one day after the wounds scabbed over. However, either that day didn't come, or I wasn't aware of its coming. Until this moment I had never allowed myself the luxury of wallowing in self-compassion. Now words and phrases and sentences suddenly pour out of my mouth. Indeed, they tumble out. Without order or rank. They step on each other's backs, and wedge against one another the way the hens used to tumble out of our henhouse into the yard when I was a child and opened their door in the morning.

And my tears fall even faster than my words. "I felt so betrayed, so betrayed!" I sob, uttering this word for the first time in connection with Leonard's infidelity. "So very, very betrayed." The roughness of Dennis' sweater against my cheek feels as solid and as sure as the kelpy rock behind our backs.

Between great gulping sobs, I tell Dennis that Leonard and I were not so much in love as in need of love, and in lieu of passion we had pledged each other total honesty and trust and caring. And I tell him that, in the end, despite our best intentions, our marriage died uncivilly. It had dissolved in mean words and court appropriations. But I shy away from telling him about the passive nights and unrequited flesh, both before and after the encroachment of Monica, so that when trust was broken, there was nothing worth salvaging. And I also shy away from telling him that I never entirely blamed Leonard for latching on to an ecstasy that could lift him from the ground and vault him into the sky—if, indeed, that's what Monica was able to offer him. It was the deceit—the extended deceit—that was so painful.

"But why couldn't Leonard have told me himself? I thought we had the kind of relationship that would permit honesty," I wail to Dennis, as though he would have an inkling as to why Leonard had kept the tryst a secret. "And if he had wanted out, why didn't he just get out? Why did he have to pick away at me for all of those months, angry at me because I wasn't her and angry at me because he found it necessary to go through the untidiness of a divorce?"

I look into Dennis' eyes and see mirrored in them the sadness that I'm certain is in my own. "It's hard to understand people's motives," he says, and in Leonard's defence adds, "But there's really no good way to do a dastardly deed." He explains. "If Leonard had come back after his first meeting with this woman and said that he'd like your permission to keep on seeing her to find out whether the relationship was going to develop into anything further, would you have agreed?"

"Of course not," I retort, annoyed that he seems to be walking the line between Leonard's team and my own. "What kind of fool do you take me for? I'm not exactly the type to sit around passively while I'm being cuckolded."

Dennis gently squeezes my shoulder. "Not on your life. Not my Tessie. But that's exactly my point. It's the motive for the deceit. It buys time," he explains. "And it was precisely because he cared about you that he would blame you for what was happening. He probably felt rotten about the deceit and he had to justify what he was doing by finding fault with you." Dennis gives me a wide grin. "At least that's how Father Freud sees it anyway. But what Dennis Walsh can't understand is why you didn't have any suspicions. Why you never questioned his trips to Toronto."

I had tried unsuccessfully to explain this same thing to my friends and I now repeat to Dennis what I had said to them. "It is easy to be duped when you trust. I believed Leonard when he said he had taken the car to the garage, gotten a raise, won this case or that case, so why shouldn't I have believed him when he told me he was going to Toronto because of business with the parent firm?"

"You're right and I'm sorry," Dennis says contritely. "I should have understood. You can't compartmentalize trust. It's all or nothing."

I reach down and pull his arm tighter around me. I need his touch at this very moment to confirm me. I need his touch to confirm that there once was a Tessie who believed in truth and honesty and unicorns and water sprites and that kamikaze moths feel no pain when they smash themselves against naked light bulbs. And I need his touch to confirm that there once was a Martin, a Carmel and a Bertha. But above all, I need his touch to confirm that I'm lovable, even if, out of guilt over his illicit liaison, Leonard tried to tell me otherwise.

Dennis and I huddle together, arms around each other, until the waves tongue at our feet and the gulls leave for home. When I notice that the light is disappearing, I shuffle myself back to being Mademoiselle Candidate, and haul my sweater sleeve across my face to wipe it dry, uncaring that the right-minded people lining my parlour walls are probably shuddering with disgust.

"If I'm not home by the time Frank gets back there'll be a search party sent out," I tell Dennis, swiping my eyes and moving out of his embrace. "He'll think Dolph coerced you into kidnapping me." I feel sheepish in the aftermath of my crying spell. I've embarrassed myself with my outburst and I've probably embarrassed Dennis too.

Dennis reaches out and pulls me back toward him so that I am once again safe in the crook of his arm. He pushes away strands of hair from my forehead and eyes, his fingers brushing my skin with a fleeting, feather-light pressure. His touch is at once innocent and intimate and I want to stay forever in the comfort of his embrace.

Dennis, too, must feel the tension because he says abruptly, changing the mood, "Remember me? Marrying, burying, unburdening and dumping-upon Dennis."

From the shelter of his arm I look out at a blood-red sun dropping into the ocean, signalling another fine day tomorrow. Striving for a tone that is as playful as his, I reply, "Well actually, I only remember the unburdening and dumping-upon Dennis. The marrying and burying fellow came after my time."

§

When I come abreast of my house on my return from the beach, I notice that Bill Curran's car is parked beside the porch door. This morning Frank told us that Bill had arrived late last night from his trip to Corner Brook and that he wouldn't be coming to headquarters until well after lunch. As soon as I open the back door, loud voices reach me from the dining room. Indeed, Bill, Greg and Frank are in such a heated argument, they don't hear me even when I enter the kitchen.

Greg is shouting, his voice surprisingly strident. "I'm totally against it, Bill. Completely and totally against it. It's outrageous even to consider it. And if we're not careful we'll find ourselves caught up in a libel suit." His voice drops a little, in keeping with the seriousness of his next statement. "I hope you realize that we're operating here on *prima facie* evidence only."

"Oh cut out the legal horseshit, Greg." Frank's voice is even louder than Greg's as he intervenes on Bill's behalf. "I think Bill's on the right track. I think we should let this leak out. Like Bill says, we know the names of the people who were tangled up in the mess. Not like we're hauling the whole thing out of thin air or anything. And it sure as hell will help us on polling day."

Greg angrily shoves his chair back from the table and I know he has forgotten about the close quarters between his chair and Grandmother's oversized china cabinet because there is a loud thump of wood against wood.

"I'm out of here!" he states, his voice loud enough to be heard outdoors. I give a quick glance into the porch to see if anyone from the community has come in. I'm thankful it is empty.

"I want no part of this conversation," Greg shouts. "Do whatever you want. But let it go on the record that I'm against it."

I walk into the dining room just as Greg is giving Frank and Bill a final admonition.

"And before you do anything about exposing Dolph's past," he says, wagging a finger first at Bill and then at Frank, "run it by Tess. She should be told what you're up to. And if you don't do it, I will!"

I act as though I have just arrived and haven't overheard any part of the argument. "What's going on?" I ask, with feigned innocence. "What should I be told?"

Instantly the room is filled with fluster. Frank, who is sitting in my seat on the opposite side of the table from Greg, gets up. To hide his confusion, he rams his hands in his pockets and jangles his loose change.

"Nothing to worry your head about," he says, fabricating on the spot. "Things are just costing a little more than we expected. But it's not such a helluva problem and we'll be able to cover the shortfall. Out of our own pockets if necessary."

Bill Curran is leaning against the far wall. He quickly straightens up and starts to leave the room to go back to his desk in the pantry. Over his shoulder, he parrots Frank. "Nothing at all. Nothing to get worked up about."

"Tell her!" Greg snaps, glaring at Bill's back and stopping him in his tracks. "Tell her or I will!" Greg, who is now standing by the china cabinet, gestures to me to take his chair. "Sit here, Tess. There are things you should hear."

He doesn't wait for Bill's response, but immediately leaves the room, brushing past me as I move toward his chair. Bill resumes his original position by the wall.

"Well?" I say, forcing a calm and controlled exterior, although I can barely contain my fury at their attempt at duplicity. I look from Bill to Frank. "Well?"

Bill gives a disgusted nod towards the doorway, just as if Greg's aura still hovers there. "Don't mind him," he says, waving his arms wildly. "Everything is lawshit with him. Lawshit this. Lawshit that. And now he has to get you all worked up over nothing."

In Greg's defence, I now feel compelled to disclose I know more about what is being covered up than either Bill or Frank think I do. Although my voice is controlled, the anger is still audible in my words.

"I was in the kitchen listening for quite awhile before I came in here," I confess. "I heard the argument. *All of it*! So don't blame Greg because he forced you to tell me what you should have told me of your own accord." I give Frank a long, level look. "What I would have expected to be told."

Both men are discomfitted. Bill shifts his position against the wall and Frank sits back down in my chair. He tosses some sheets of looseleaf towards Greg's end of the table. Then, as if he realizes he is cornered, he says in exasperation, "Oh for the love of Christ, tell her! We might as well, because if we don't *that* arsehole will."

He tosses his pencil across the table so that it lands on the sheets of looseleaf near Greg's side of the table. "To think I was the one who proposed him for campaign manager. A royal arsehole that's what he is.

When something gets stuck in his craw, there's no way you can dislodge it."

Bill gives me a disgruntled look and then says in an off-handed way, as if Greg, as usual, is making mountains out of molehills, "I found out some smut on Dolph when I was away and Greg thinks we shouldn't use it. He's got some bee up his arse about us being slapped with a lawsuit."

He immediately begins telling the story, predicting that its exposure will be the downfall of Dolph. His telling is so pat that I surmise he spent most of the drive home getting the sentences together in just the right order.

"Well, you see, girl, I met this fellow in Corner Brook and naturally enough we got talking about the election." Bill savours the telling, and every now and again he pauses to rub his back up against the wall. He looks like a sheep rubbing against a rock and I almost expect to see clumps of wool clinging to the chair rail. "So I brought up Dolph's name." He waits an instant to let this sink in. "Well, sir, you should have seen this fellow's ears perk up." Bill slices his hands along the sides of his own ears. "Yessir, those ears of his shot straight up like a dog's when there's a noise in the dead of night, and then he up and asks me whether it is the same Dolph Simmons that he knows."

Bill nods towards Frank, "So like I told Frank, I give out what information I have and sure enough our Dolph is one and the same. Well sir, then he up and tells me that Dolph is as crooked as a ram's horn."

Again Bill rubs the small of his back against the chair rail, repeating, "Yes sir, as crooked as a ram's horn."

He then goes on to relate how Dolph had an insurance business with many clients from down the bay, people who were unsophisticated and too trusting. These clients usually gave Dolph cash premiums, which as often as not he pocketed. Since the people didn't ask for a receipt, he had always managed to persuade them that they only *thought* they had paid up whenever they received notice from head office of delinquent payment. Of course they always paid a second time. Sometimes too, when the clients had extra money, they would pay two premiums at once, but only one of the premiums would be forwarded to head office. Of course, Dolph had to keep diligent records because he couldn't risk hitting on the same client more than once. As Bill points out, even fools wise up after awhile.

Bill continues, saying that sometimes Dolph simply robbed Peter to pay Paul and used one client's premium to pay off another client's premium—especially a premium that was coming close to due date. But, despite the complicated book work, Dolph always managed to stay a jump ahead of being discovered—or at least he did, until a client died suddenly without giving Dolph enough time to juggle his records. The client's widow was told she couldn't collect on her husband's insurance because his policy had lapsed on account of late payment of the premium. However, this woman had always conscientiously marked the day and the hour of payment on her calendar and she knew she had indeed given Dolph the money.

Once the investigation got underway, Dolph's scheme totally disintegrated, but because the insurance company didn't want the news getting around that they had a salesman who was a crook, they agreed to hush up the incident on the condition they would recover full payment of delinquent monies. According to Bill's source, Dolph's parents were the ones who paid up and they were well able to do so because there were pots of money in the Simmons family. Bill's source has also told him that Dolph had gotten into financial trouble because he had his grandfather's gambling streak in him. With Dolph's grandfather, it was outsmarting the customs boats when he was rumrunning between St. Pierre and Boston. With Dolph, it was horse racing and poker games.

As Bill tells it, after the incident was hushed up, Dolph was sent to the Mainland to get "the cure." He returned home a couple of years later, after his father died and left enough money for him to set up the grocery store business in the Cove.

Bill adds his own touch to the story, stating that Eileen Walsh knew the minute she laid eyes on Dolph that he was the perfect match for her daughter Sarah. He says, "He was a bit of a dandy—the hoity-toity type Eileen fancied—and his pocketful of cash made him even more suitable." Bill hypothesizes that so far Dolph has never reverted to pattern because Sarah always looks after the books for his business and never affords him the opportunity to do anything underhanded. But, of course, this situation could change when Dolph gets into government because Sarah will no longer be in a position to police him.

After the telling, Bill is exhausted. He pulls out a chair and lowers himself into it.

"Well?" he says, giving me an anxious look, like a child who thinks he has done something good and can't understand why the deed isn't looked upon in such a light. "Well? Don't you agree we should let it be known? Don't you?"

Frank looks at me too, but says nothing, although I can hear him hauling in his breath, waiting for my reaction. When I entered the dining room it was filled with fluster. Now it fills with stillness. I can almost hear the waiting.

"Well! What do you think?" Bill prods. "I can have it spread around within the hour. The sooner it gets out, the surer our win." When I don't answer, he prods again. "Well? What do you think?"

I get up and pace the few steps between the china

cabinet and the door. As I walk back and forth across the linoleum floor, my toes curl into the soles of my shoes as if they are searching for something to hold onto, as if they are digging for solid ground.

What *do* I think? I think Greg should have stayed around to give me support. I think I don't have the killer instinct that seems to be necessary for this job that I'm spending almost twenty-four hours a day trying to get. I think Dennis could help me if only Dolph weren't his brother-in law.

Frank's impatient voice cuts into my thoughts. "Like Bill says, if we're going to get it out there, it has to be done while there's time for it to do some good. It would sew this thing up for us. We'd have it in the bag. Like they say, we're making great inroads, but making inroads is one hell of a far cry from being out in front."

I suck in my breath and I can almost taste the victory that Bill and Frank are prophesying for me. I can see myself, me, Tess Corrigan, Member of the House of Assembly, taking her oath of office, and I'm surprised at my greediness for this job. And right behind that taste of victory, is the sweet, yet bitter as gall, taste of sure revenge. I think of Sarah Walsh and how I used to fantasize about getting even with her when I grew up and became so powerful that she would be grovelling at my feet for mercy.

The years fall away and once more I hear Sarah singing the skipping rope song that she had revamped to taunt me about my bigamist father. Pain, razor sharp, slices through my whole being as her voice slides easily over the lines that were ever-after indelibly imprinted on my soul. *"Tessie Corrigan is no good. Cut her up for fi-re wood. Spoons, cups, forks and knives, her Yankee father had two wives."* As soon as the words are finished, another revamping of the song flashes into my mind, but this time the words aren't sodden with my pain. Instead, they are sodden with the pain of Dolph's children. I can almost see their eyes glistening with unshed tears. I can almost hear their voices, hoarse from sobbing. *"Randolph's children are no good. Cut them up for fi-re wood. Cups and saucers on a hook, their Tory father is a crook."*

I stop my pacing in mid-step and look from Frank to Bill. "We can't let that information get out." My voice is sure and deliberate. "In fact, it's not going to leave this room! Not while I have any say about it!"

Frank is the first to react. He shouts explosively, "Jesus H. Christ, Tess. I'd like to know why not!" He slaps the table to bring me to my senses. "Shit girl, we've got the goods on Dolph and I for one say we should run with it. It'll tie up this election for us."

Bill gives Frank a look that is full of sneer. "What did I tell ya. She's so green she doesn't know why we're in this racket. Thinks we're in it for the good of our health."

He turns to address me, the sneer replaced with condescension. "My love, you've been listening to too much of that lawshit stuff Greg Slade's tried to shovel into you. He's addled your brain so you can't think straight."

My anger leaps upward with a furious rush, although I manage to keep my voice calm. "It has nothing to do with lawsuits, Bill. Nothing at all. If we destroy Dolph, we'll destroy his children and I would have thought *even you* would hold the line on destroying innocent children."

Bill retaliates by placing his hand over his heart and looking heavenward, with a mockingly beneficent look on his face.

"What have we here, Lord? A candidate for the Liberals or a candidate for sainthood? No more idea than the Man in the Moon what's needed to win an election." He walks past me out to the kitchen as if he can't bear to be in the same room with such a dilettante.

Exasperated, I look at Frank, searching for some

sign of the humanity I once believed was part of him. "Winning isn't worth that price. Is it Frank?"

Because he doesn't answer immediately, I prod. "You know very well it isn't."

But Frank knows nothing of the kind. "For the love of Christ, Tess, don't talk nonsense. 'Tis all about winning. What I know or don't know has nothing to do with it." The muscles in his jaw work at controlling his anger. He pauses for a moment and then whispers out of the side of his mouth, low enough so Bill, who is still in the kitchen, can't hear. "Sure you're not holding off on account of the Holy Father? Are you sure that's not the motive behind all of this."

I sink into Greg's chair, too beaten even to deny Frank's accusation. But Frank knows he has gone too far because he instantly reaches across the table and presses my hand.

"Christ, girl. I'm sorry. Shouldn't have said that." He speaks heavily, his words weighted with regret. "That wasn't called fer."

He shakes his head, perplexed. "I don't know what this election is doing to us all."

I shake my head, too. I think of the many times Frank and I sat at his kitchen table and bantered with one another while we sampled Rose's pea soup and partridge-berry pie. The same thoughts must have run through his mind, because he now says in a sad voice, "God Almighty, girl, we're forgettin' we used to be friends. Forgettin' we used to be civilized."

He faces out toward the kitchen and shouts to Bill, but in a tone that is meant to be mollifying. "Bill, can't you see? She's right. We can't be responsible for destroying those children. Probably the marriage, too, because I'm not sure how much of this Sarah knows. And I sure as hell can't have a broken marriage on my conscience." After that absolving statement, Frank dusts off his hands as if he is Pontius Pilate. "But boy, I can't muzzle you. If you're hell bent on telling it, tell it. I just can't be part of it, that's all I'm saying."

But Bill isn't moved to benevolence. He comes back into the dining room and stands ramrod straight against the wall. The full brunt of his anger settles in his face as he addresses Frank.

"So she's converted you, too. Before this is over we'll have to canonize the whole jeesless lot of you." His eyes sweep the room, giving recognition to the loss of Frank's support, and including Greg in the conversation. "Well, you three aren't running the whole show here. Like you said, you can't muzzle me. And there are others involved as well. Others with a stake in this election. They'll certainly agree with me that we should spread this around."

He gives me a look that says I have no business being in politics anyway, and again he sneers, "In case you don't know it, my love, we're not in this racket to qualify for sainthood or anything. Father Damian we're not. This is politics. Not ministering to the lepers. Nor are we playing skipping rope or cubby house!"

He throws my lack of experience in my face. "Then again, perhaps you don't know." His voice is snide. "You never paid your dues in the party like others before you. Just came in as raw as a March day."

I take a deep breath to gain control of myself, knowing that if I am to exert my will over Bill, it has to be done at this very moment. I make eye contact with him and forbid myself even to blink. My heart is trembling like a leaf in a summer gale.

"Bill," I say slowly and deliberately, as though every word must be heard, and heard the first time, "If one whisper of this story of yours gets out before the election, I'll bow out of the race immediately. You'll have to call it quits." I pause, to let this sink in and then add, still holding his eyes, "And if that happens, the Tories will win by default and you'll never get that gravel pit contract you've got your eye on."

While I still have my nerve revved up, I quickly tack on a rider. "And if you spread it about after the election, I'll discredit you. And Greg will too. We'll say you wanted that gravel pit job so badly, you went nosing around for dirt and you didn't care whether it was true or false."

Silence thunders in the room, filling every crevice. I'm just as shocked as Frank and Bill at the words that just rolled off my lips and, like them, I know I mean what I said. Mutely, we look at each other.

Bill is the first to muster composure. He pushes past me and rushes from the room, hesitating in the kitchen only long enough to throw out a slur.

"Goddamn petticoat candidate! What else can you expect! Let the crooks take over the government. Put the fox in with the chickens. No skin off my arse." He gives the porch door a vicious slam, leaving his words to trail after him like slimy creatures from a swamp.

By the time Frank regains his composure, Grandmother's dishes have settled down in the china cabinet.

"You know girl," he says, almost off-handedly, "Bill's got a point there. About the fox. This Dolph thing places us in a bit of a bind, don't you think?" He taps his pencil against the papers on the table in front of him and repeats softly, "A bit of a bind indeed."

We both discuss this new predicament. I admit I haven't thought about the repercussions that could arise if a Member who has a previous inclination towards gambling or misusing public funds gets into office. But in Dolph's case, I believe the issue is only an academic one and I tell Frank so.

"I can't see how it puts us in much of a bind, Frank. After all, Dolph won't be in a position to jeopardize the province. He'll only be a member of the opposition. No opportunity for power. And besides, his indiscretions took place almost fifteen years ago. I think he's proved himself over the years."

"Maybe so and maybe not so," Frank says with his usual deliberation. "Like Bill pointed out, maybe the opportunity hasn't come his way. And from where I sit, once a gambler always a gambler. And besides, who is to say that in the upcoming general election—and that's not too far off—the PCs won't get in and then for sure he'll be in the position of the fox."

Frank gets up from the table, looking as weary as I feel. "Damned if we do and damned if we don't," he says. "Nothing is cut and dried. My advice is that we all sleep on this before we decide to crack it open or shove it under the rug. It's like Greg said before you came in. What's to say spreading this dirt won't backfire on us. It may turn sympathy towards Dolph. We have to be damn careful about that. And that's something Bill doesn't seem to understand."

He moves toward the kitchen door and speaks to me over his shoulder as he leaves the dining room. "I'll catch up with Bill. Going off half-cocked like he did, there's no guarantee what he'll do. I'll tell him we're going to sleep on it. And I'll get him to see the possibility of it being turned back on us. That's the thing to do. We'll all sleep on it."

I am certain the night is going to last forever until finally I look out the window and see the sun hoisting itself above the trees. I get up immediately, abandoning all pretense of sleep. Frank's telephone call comes just as I am lighting the kitchen fire. He tells me that he and Greg are on their way to my place so that we can get the

Dolph situation out of the way before the business day begins—and before Bill arrives.

I have the coffee brewing by the time they arrive and as soon as we sit down at the table we begin the discussion. It turns out that I'm not the only one who had a sleepless night. Both Greg and Frank have spent the night like me—going over options, limited though they are. The three of us have no difficulty agreeing on how the situation is to be handled. Dolph must be told that we know what we know, but that we will withhold this information unless we are ever given a reason to disclose it. We all believe that if Dolph knows that we are in possession of this information, it will be enough to curb him should he ever be in a position to abuse public funds. And this course of action may be enough to appease Bill and his cohorts, so there will be no need to make a public issue of it. Frank is sure it will be enough for Bill, especially now that Bill understands about the probability of the disclosure backfiring on us. As well, Frank says he told Bill last night that I would indeed concede the election if the word got out.

By a concensus of two, I am given the job of talking with Dolph.

§

Arranging a meeting with my PC opponent isn't as easy as we anticipated. He, understandably, doesn't want to be seen coming to my headquarters, and for similar political reasons, I don't want to meet him at his. Nor do I want to go to his house and risk the chance of running into Dennis and Sarah. After much back-and-forth discussion, we agree to meet in St. John's in two days. Both of us have to be in the city on business then. We settle on the waterfront restaurant at the back of Bowerings Department Store.

By the time I arrive at the restaurant, Dolph has already smoked a half pack of cigarettes. The ashtray is over-flowing with cigarette stubs and broken matchsticks and the cellophane wrapping from a newly-opened package of *Menthols*.

When I come to his table Dolph makes a feeble at-tempt at conventional niceties and beckons me to sit op-posite him. As I pull out a chair and settle into it, he eyes me ferally—back arched, head lifted, eyes statue-still—as if he smells danger, as if he senses that disaster is drifting in through The Narrows on a late spring wind. He begins to protect himself as best he can, erecting a physical barrier between us with the ashtray, placing it and its loaded contents in the center of the table.

He glances at his watch and says churlishly, as if I am the one whose unsavoury past is about to come to light, "I don't have all day to waste on you. So whatever nonsense you have to say about my insurance business in Corner Brook, get on with it."

He plucks the partly-smoked cigarette out of his mouth, douses it in the ashtray and immediately lights up another one, pocketing the half-empty package of *Menthols* in a way that says he won't be needing it again because this encounter will only last as long as the cigarette in his mouth.

I strive for Greg Slade's type of calm control as I methodically lay my purse on the table and pull my chair in closer. I catch the waitress' eye and ask for a pot of coffee.

"It isn't nonsense, Dolph," I say coolly and in my own time. "We know, proof positive, that you were in-volved with some crooked shenanigans with your in-surance business."

I look for some reaction, and finding none, continue

to build my case. "As a matter of fact, we know your father bought you off. Otherwise, you'd have done time in the penitentiary."

Dolph swallows hard and busies himself with his tie before starting to bluster. "Bullshit! All bullshit! You're just trying to get me rattled, hoping it'll slow down my campaigning."

I toss out the name of the man whose death had brought Dolph's scheming to an end. "Hazen Hodder," I say, eyes watchful. "Does that name ring any bells with you?"

Dolph lurches forward in his chair as if he has been hit from behind. Fear flushes in his face, his jaw muscles tighten, and he jerks his hands from the table as though he has dropped cigarette ash on them. He pulls the cigarette out of his mouth and fumbles in the ashtray for space to butt it. Cellophane wrapping and cigarette stubs overflow on the table. He attempts to reposition the mess, but his hands are shaking so much he can't get the garbage to stay humped in one pile. He gives up the effort and laces his fingers together as if to cage them in one place so they can't betray him with their trembling.

"Who else knows?" he asks, his shoulders slumping and his whole stance capitulating. All of his arrogance is suddenly of no more substance than the smoke that is wafting up from the ashtray. "Who else besides you?"

"Most of the Committee." I name names. "But we've agreed to sit on the information unless you ever give us cause to do otherwise."

He burrows his head in his hands, and his body seems to fall in upon itself. "Please don't tell anyone," he mumbles. "For the love of God, don't let this get out. It would kill Sarah. She knows nothing about it. I thought what was in the past was in the past."

He raises his head and for the first time since our meeting looks directly at me, his sincerity so blatant it is unnerving. "I'd be willing to withdraw from the election rather than have the family destroyed. I'd come up with some excuse. I'd do anything not to hurt them."

I immediately break his gaze and focus on the ashtray so he won't be able to see the pity in my eyes. "We'll use it only if we ever have to, Dolph. Only if it comes to that."

He unclasps his hands and I can see the white pressure spots on his fingers. "You won't ever have to, Tess. As God is my judge, you won't ever have to."

I believe him.

We talk for a few minutes longer and when I get up to leave, Dolph tries to pull the moment together, tries to shake things back into place. He forces a pale smile. "I'm really grateful, Tess. If there's ever anything I can do ... If there's anything ..."

I leave the table and walk across the room to the stairs that lead from the restaurant to the main part of the store. Just before I take the first step down, I glance back over my shoulder. Dolph is still at the table, staring down at the mess. One hand is holding a newly-lit cigarette, the other is rubbing his forehead. He looks so woebegone, I have to stifle an urge to go to him and tell him he has no worries about exposure; that it is also to our advantage to keep this information under wraps. Thanks, however, to my recently acquired political astuteness, I am able to hold my compassion in check. I quickly turn to face the stairs and I head outdoors.

Dennis and I have shared time together on many occasions since our first meeting at the beach. Usually we meet for lunch and always at the beach. In between our meetings we talk on the telephone. But when I'm not with him and when I haven't been talking to him on the telephone, I am always thinking about him.

Today, Saturday, we have arranged another luncheon date. We have chosen the beach again, because by going through the short-cut at the back of my house, we can get to and from our sheltered spot without being seen and without bringing on unwanted tongue-wagging. Because we close down the headquarters from noon until one, I never have to explain my absence or whereabouts during this time. Today, though, because there are only three days left before we go to the polls, the headquarters is in total frenzy and I'm worried about being able to get away at all, much less being able to get away unnoticed. The phone hasn't stopped ringing all morning: voters are making enquiries about absentee ballots and about names not appearing on the voting list; there are questions from poll workers about rules and regulations governing polling stations; and there are calls from drivers offering to take voters to the polls on election day.

By five past twelve, when Greg, the only person who hasn't already left for lunch, looks at his watch and mumbles, "Where did the morning go?" I'm practically panic-stricken. When he leaves, I don't even take time to change into clothes that would be suitable for the trek to the beach, but dash off for the short-cut over the cliff still dressed in my white cotton skirt, and sandals that are little more than straps and soles. I hurry along the path, pushing branches out of my way and stepping over rocks, no longer finding them as troublesome as I did in the beginning. June is usually a bad month in the Cove, but today the sun is shining brightly and the air is heavy with the scent of lilacs in full bloom, mixed with the smell of freshly-broken ground.

When I come to the end of the path, just before I have to leap over the piece of cliff that will land me on the beach, I stop and look around. Dennis is already sitting in the landwash, staring out to sea, waiting for me. He is dressed in khaki-coloured pants and a black-and-white checked shirt, with the sleeves rolled up almost to his elbows. His hair, as always, is flopping over his forehead and in the sunlight it is the same colour as the wet sand that rims the landwash. He has his guitar slung over his shoulder, keeping good his promise that today we will sing songs like we used to do.

Sandpipers are bobbing about here and there on the sand and a pair of them walk past Dennis as if he poses no threat. They walk briskly, looking directly forward and nodding their heads every so often as if in whispered conversation. I'm reminded of nuns going to chapel. My memory supplies the swish of rosary beads and the rustle of serge habits along still corridors.

I look out over the ocean. The tide is lazier than I've ever seen it; the waves barely make it to shore. There is just enough of a breeze to keep the fog high over the water, and if I focus really hard, I can see all the way to the opposite shore—that magical place where, as a child, I believed the sun dropped down every evening. I used to watch from our kitchen window as the ball of blood-red sun dipped out of sight, and landed, I was sure, in the landwash surrounding Fox Harbour.

After a few minutes, Dennis senses my presence and looks in my direction. He quickly scrambles to his feet and comes to help me down over the cliff. All of the nearby gulls and sandpipers scatter out of the way, but they regroup again the instant he runs from the spot.

When he reaches the base of the cliff, he holds up his arms so I can ease into them. Usually, we break apart the instant my feet are on solid ground, each of us always acutely aware of the invisible line in the sand that separates us and over which we know we must never trespass. Apart from that first day when Dennis put his arms around me to comfort me after I had talked about the breakdown of my marriage, we have had no physical contact, other than the occasional accidental touch of a hand, or the fleeting brush of a shoulder. This lack of contact has come about by mutual, although unspoken, consent. It is as if both of us are intuitively protecting the other from what could be unbearable pain. Sometimes, though, our need to touch, to embrace, to kiss, is so present that its scent hovers in the air as sweet and as heady as the blooms of the lilac trees, and we have difficulty manoeuvring ordinary conversation in and around this neediness.

"I'm so glad you're here," Dennis says now, and surprises me by holding me a moment longer than usual, a moment longer than necessary. When we break apart he tells me, as though he had been preparing himself for disappointment, that he was worried I wouldn't come.

"I know things are pushing in on you just now with the election so close. I was afraid you wouldn't be able to get away." He tosses his hair from his forehead as he talks and when he looks at me, his eyes confirm the depth of the disappointment he would feel if I couldn't get away.

I readily admit my own desire to be with him. "I was afraid, too," I say and add more softly than I intended to, "But I'm glad I'm here."

He reaches out his arm as though to encircle my waist, and then, as if remembering, lets it drop to his side. We walk in silence to the spot he has already picked out. He explains, as he points to the blanket splayed out and surrounded now by gulls, that because it is such a beautiful day he saw no need to go to our usual sheltered place.

When we settle down on the blanket we sit close, so close that our shoulders frequently touch. We carry on small talk, our thin words covering the meaningful conversation that is couched in the silences between our words. We start with politics although, as usual, because of Dennis' divided loyalties, this is a short-lived subject. We discuss the magnificence of the weather and the proper time for putting in turnip plants and if people actually do eat parsnips after they get old enough to make their own food choices.

When a gull comes too close to the bag of sandwiches I have brought with me, we both reach out to brush it away and our hands meet. Dennis' eyes find mine and we exchange a look so soft that we have to hurriedly turn away. We discover that both of us watched last night's fiery sunset dip into the sea, he from his bedroom, I from mine. Each of us sighs. When Dennis says he hasn't slept well for the last few nights because he has a lot on his mind that needs sorting out, I reply, so low I can barely be heard above the breeze, "I know. Me too."

To break the tension that is building around us, Dennis reaches for his guitar and slips the strap over his shoulder. He begins singing *If I Were a Blackbird*. After he finishes the first verse, old patterns resume and I join in hither and yon. In our adolescence, whenever we came upon soulful lines sodden with private meaning, we would harmonize, gazing into each other's eyes as though never in all of history had such insurmountable obstacles been placed in the path of two lovers. My eyes now find Dennis' and together we sing the words that, for us, had always contained the disapproval of both our families.

My Lover is handsome
In every degree
But my parents despise him because he loves me.

I'm just about to begin the last line of the verse when suddenly and without warning, voices from yesterday force their way into my mind, crowding out the song. The first voice is Grandmother's, confused and bewildered. The voice of Grandmother when I was seventeen.

"Tessie Corrigan! Tessie Corrigan! Don't you

know what you're up against, girl? Don't you realize what you're doing? The gates of hell will surely prevail against you if you stop him from becoming a priest."

Then comes Eileen's voice—the voice of Dennis' doting mother—its stridency tempered by her son's gentle editing; its content re-formed and interpreted from my own jaundiced perspective.

"Now you listen to me, Dennis Walsh, my Holy Orders, All Hallows-bound son!" I can see Eileen wagging an admonishing finger at seventeen-year-old Dennis. "How can you risk your vocation on account of Tessie Corrigan? And my dear boy, even if you weren't considering All Hallows, she still isn't for you. Don't you know her father was a bigamist and her uncle a lapsed? And that Bertha can try and convince someone else, but not me, because no matter how hard she wants to put a different face on it, I know Martin died a lapsed. Lived a lapsed. Died a lapsed."

And once again comes Grandmother's voice, this time hoping guilt will do what logic and persuasion had so far failed to do.

"And God Almighty, Tessie, if on account of stopping Dennis Walsh from the priesthood, *you* don't make it up above, I'll be up there practically all by myself."

Grandmother is standing in the middle of the kitchen floor, her face clouded by memories from her own yesterdays; her voice heavy with fearful possibilities—possibilities she had not dared share with anyone but me. Possibilities she could read years ago in Eileen Walsh's eyes.

"Your mother will be up there with me when her time comes. No doubt about that, Tessie girl. I'll certainly have her for company. But we know your Grandfather, Poor Ned, didn't get far. Him doin' away with himself. And then there's Poor Martin, God help me, me only son, the Lord have mercy on his soul. I often wonders where he got to." She pauses, sighs heavily and then continues. "Yes girl, so often I wonders about that. Such a good boy." A flicker of a smile crosses her face when she recalls her scampish son. "Oh a bit of a scallawag, of course. But there's worse things. I prays every night before I lays down me head that Father Kelley wasn't making up a story just to give me some peace of mind."

As if she suddenly remembers that I'm present and she is weary from constantly having to remind me not to take tales out of the house, even though I'm now half grown, her face folds itself into sterness and her voice takes on hard resolve.

"But never a word outside this kitchen about that! Never a word Tessie Corrigan! Just because I know Poor Martin died lapsed no matter what Father Kelley said is no reason for the rest of the Cove to know." She explains why she has chosen to keep this secret to herself. "I wasn't going to take any chances with him not getting a Christian burial. Him a sight better Christian than them who'd wag their tongues if they knew the rights of things."

And then, while still standing in the centre of the floor, her eyes darken and she pulls her forehead into anxious lines as she looks up at the smoke-smudged kitchen ceiling. She points upwards, beyond the ceiling, to her bedroom and to the wooden crucifix that is hanging on a wall over the head of her bed. A white alabaster Jesus is suspended from that crucifix, and bitter red blood is dripping from five cruel wounds and congealing into carved roses at the Sacred Feet.

"Don't ever be the cause of one trickle of blood from those wounds, Tessie Corrigan!" she chastises. "Hear me, girl. Not *one* trickle. I've got enough to do to make amends on Poor Martin's behalf, let alone having to go to bat for you."

I try to make yesterday's voices fade by concentrating on the song, forcing myself to sing louder than usual.

If I were a blackbird
I'd whistle and sing
I'd follow the ship
that ... my true love ... sails in

But my voice falters and the words lie trembling on my lips. Tears smart my eyes. I jump up and rush to the edge of the landwash as if the placid tide will cleanse me of this unsanctified love that I have for Dennis—this unlawful passion that is raging inside me; this passion that can no longer be cloaked as friendship.

"What is it, Tessie?" Dennis asks anxiously, rushing to my side. He places a concerned arm around my shoulder. "You're trembling. Like a leaf. What's happened?"

I step aside. Away from his touch. "Nothing," I mumble. "Nothing." I stare at the sand, not trusting myself to look at him.

Dennis pulls me close again as if it is the most natural act in the world and this time I offer no resistance. In the gentle breeze, my hair blows around my face, and he smoothes his hand over it, coaxing it back into place.

After a few silent moments, he asks softly, his voice so tender it is as though he is comforting a young child, "Are you in love with me Tessie? Is that what's the matter?"

I jerk myself erect, my body stiffening with denial. Seconds later, I stammer, "What ...? Of course not ... I ... Ridiculous!"

I'm about to continue, to say that I don't know where he got such an outrageous notion, but the words stick in my mouth, refusing to form into more lies.

I tear myself from his embrace, as if only by rupturing the gentleness and softness surrounding me can I let out the horrible truth. Angry words form in my heart and roll off my lips so easily that I'm sure they've been hovering close by for several days.

"You're right. I am in love with you. I am! I am!" My tone is blaming, as if he is at fault. "And it's not fair. Not twice in one lifetime."

The anger quickly turns into sobs and I bury my face in my hands. Dennis reaches out and pulls me back into his arms and presses his face against my hair.

"I know you love me, Tessie," he says tenderly. "I've known it for some time. It's as plain as day in your eyes." He pauses and the words that he speaks next seem to be wrenched from his soul. "And the reason I can see it there is because I love you. I love you very, very much. And I not only love you. I'm in love with you."

In the aftermath of this admission, I become aware of silence. Hushed silence. Even the breeze seems to be holding its breath. A seagull stops grappling over a dead fish and cocks its head sideways, a questioning look on its face as though it heard Dennis' admission and can hardly believe its own ears. The tide just lolls on the landwash, making no move to draw back out to sea. For several seconds we stay wrapped in this stillness, until more words, words even more awesome, shatter it.

"I'm going to leave the priesthood, Tessie. That's what I meant when I said I haven't been sleeping much. I've been trying to sort things out."

Leave the priesthood! I flinch as if a jagged rock has pierced my flesh. My bare arms become covered in goosebumps and I rub them to get out the chill—a chill that seems to be covering my soul as well. The silence of an instant ago is immediately shattered. The tide pulls away from the shore with a harsh sucking noise. The seagull goes back to grappling over the maggoty fish and the cold wind cuts into my bare flesh before it grabs up an armful of fog and plucks it in over the beach, in towards the Cove.

I yank my arms from around Dennis' body and step back so that I'm facing him. My voice rises until it is higher than the wind. "No! You can't," I shout. "No you can't! My God Almighty, you can't." My whole being recoils as the word "defrocked" slashes through my mind. The word gets bigger and bigger until my skull aches from the burden of containing it. Defrocked! DEFROCKED! DEFROCKED! Other words, words I mumbled with humdrum familiarity as I followed along with Sr. Clarence in her prayer for vocations, bottleneck up behind "defrocked" and push it out of the way. *Come, Holy Spirit, fill the hearts of Your faithful and kindle in them the fire of a vocation ...*

"No Dennis. No!" I shout. "No! You can't leave! You can't! You can't!" I shake my head so vigorously an earring drops off and buries itself in the sand. I make no attempt to retrieve it. "You can't leave! At least not on my account. I couldn't handle that. I can't be the cause of you being defrocked."

Dennis reaches for my hand and holds it in both of his. He forces me to face him. "Look at me, Tessie. Listen to me. It's not yours to handle." He speaks softly, soothingly. "It's my problem. And its up to me to square things with God, my way." He gives an easy laugh. "And I wouldn't be defrocked, as you call it. That's ancient history. Things are different since Vatican II. I'd go through channels and get permission to leave."

Even though the beach is, as usual, deserted, Dennis still suggests that we should move to our sheltered place so we can be assured of complete privacy. "We have to talk," he says. "Important talk." His calming voice reaches me as if from a great distance.

We walk along the beach, hand in hand, and when we come to our sheltered place, we spread the blanket so our backs can lean against the rock. We sit close together, and Dennis' arm cushions my shoulder. I listen as he tells me he fell back in love with me on the first night he saw me—the night of the debate.

"I've been fooling myself that it's just friendship between us, Tessie. At least on my account." His words

. 160 .

are heavy and they frame my own thoughts, my own guilts. He pours out his doubts. "And then again, maybe I didn't fall *back* in love with you that night. Maybe I never fell out of love with you. Maybe I should never have gone into the priesthood. Maybe we're fated to be together."

His voice lightens and he jogs my memory about the past. "Remember when you used to say you wished you were centred—like me, knowing what I wanted, who I wanted to become? And I would tell you not to envy me because I had two centres—you and the priesthood—and I had to make a choice between them. But when I'd say that, you'd feel even more short-changed, because I had two centres and you didn't even have one."

I remember only too well. I used to ask him how he could be so certain of what he wanted, while I was floundering like a ship in a storm, desperately searching for some place to drop anchor. I'd tell him that sometimes I wished I could head up a revolution—bloodless, of course—but I didn't know how to go about getting one underway. And I would be so jealous, because I wasn't his only centre, that I would taunt him by asking if, like St. Paul, the clouds had opened and struck him to the ground and he had heard a Voice directing him to the priesthood. He would never get angry when I carried on so spitefully. He'd just say that it wasn't like that at all. He just *knew*! *Knew in his heart*!

He tells me now about how he felt when he went back home on the night after the debate, the night of our first meeting in thirteen years. "It was just as if time had stood still." He shakes his head in wonderment. "You looked the very same. Your hair like always. And your ..." He breaks off and gives a small, shy laugh. "Don't suppose you ever knew this and now I'm almost embarrassed to say it, but I always loved the way your clothes fitted your body. The pleats in your uniform were hardly disturbed. They never gaped open or jibbed out over your hips like they did on some girls." He breaks off again, waves his hands as much as to say only an idiot would bring up this subject now. "I don't know why I'm going on with this blathering. Maybe it stops me from having to talk about important stuff."

He gets up, takes a few steps away from me, rakes his fingers through his hair. After a couple of seconds he comes back and sits down again, this time with weariness.

"Oh my God! Oh my God!" Once more, the words seem to be wrenched from his depths. "I can't pretend anymore, Tessie. I can't deceive myself any longer. God knows I've tried. But the honest truth is that ever since that night, I have wanted to be with you every minute of every hour and when I'm not with you, I'm thinking about you." Again, he rams his hands through his hair. "I'm not fit to be in the priesthood anymore."

My mind rushes backwards to a newspaper clipping sent to me by Mother years earlier and which I have read so often it is now committed to memory.

Dennis Francis Walsh, SFM, son of Thomas and Eileen Walsh, was ordained to the priesthood October 20, 1965 in the Church of St. John the Baptist. The Ordaining Bishop was the Most Reverend Allan Kierstead assisted by Very Reverend James Mulhalley, Superior General of the Scarboro Foreign Mission Society. Among those present for both the Ordination and the First Mass were Father Walsh's parents and his sister Sarah.

While I have been remembering, Dennis has been talking so I only come to his conversation after much of it has passed.

"... So you see it's not something that popped into my head a minute ago. I haven't had a full night's sleep in weeks. I've agonized and agonized over it. But with

Mother and Father dead, it makes it easier. Sarah will be hurt, of course, but she has the children and Dolph."

When he tells me he has finally wrestled his conscience into accepting a compromise—although he won't be a priest, he'll still be serving God—his mood swings upward. He launches excitedly into the new life he has dreamed for us.

"The priesthood isn't the only way to serve God, Tessie," he rationalizes. "We could both be missionaries, hopefully through the Church, but if not, then with some other organization. I mean, Jesus didn't ask what religion anyone was. He just helped wherever He saw need." Dennis' eyes shine with happy expectation. "And you could get training and then we could both serve the poor." He puts both arms around me, pulling me close and saying eagerly, "So you see, Tessie, God will be getting two for the price of one, so to speak."

I burrow my head into his shoulder and let my lips nuzzle his neck, especially the soft flesh that for years has been protected by the round Roman collar and I, too, think of the rich, fulfilling future waiting for us.

During one of our earlier meetings, Dennis had told me about a priest friend of his who was on a mission in the Philippines and who almost single-handedly had organized villagers to picket a lumber company that was destroying the forests surrounding their villages. Dennis had related how the destruction was being carried out with impunity, and how villages were being flooded, vegetation was being destroyed and wildlife was becoming endangered. He had gone on to say how this priest and a handful of villagers had barricaded the road so the lumber trucks couldn't get past them to go into the woods. In this way, they had saved their villages.

Recalling this story now, my mind sees the two of us—Dennis and me—camping out all night, lying on the road, our very lives at stake, defying the lumber trucks. I see us going into poverty-stricken huts, bringing warm blankets and food, teaching children to read, and in a pinch even delivering babies. An earlier dream of mine—a dream that took root when I left Toronto—of a house on the outskirts of St. John's, either in Kilbride or in Mount Pearl, pales in comparison. I easily toss aside the rooms that I was going to decorate in grass greens, sunlight yellows and sky blues—my frivolous wish of someday having a home filled with the appearance of year-round summer. The dusty roads of a Peruvian village now offer far more enticement. I'm even quite willing to leave the building of the community college in the Cove to Dolph. He can fill up the potholes in the roads as well, and see to it that Mrs. Benson gets electricity—although here I must admit I have a pang or two of regret because I wanted to be the one who finally gave substance to the old woman's dream.

As Dennis and I sit wrapped in each other's arms and spin our own dreams, I come to accept his decision to leave the priesthood. After all, as he pointed out, he isn't leaving God. And he isn't leaving the poor. He is just arranging for me to share this life with him. In this warm cocoon of love and caring, it is easy to cast aside such impediments to our happiness as Dennis' vows of Holy Orders and my decree of shattered matrimony.

The time passes so quickly, it is almost one-thirty when I remember to look at my watch. We say a rushed goodbye, Dennis to return home the long way around, I through the short-cut. We know it will be several days before we can meet again. Polling day is Tuesday, only three days away, and on Monday, Dennis is going to St. John's to inquire from a friend who recently left the priesthood about the procedures that need to be followed if he is to leave his order with the least amount of upheaval. We kiss when we come to the edge of my path, a gentle kiss that seals and sanctions our love and confirms the rightness of our decision.

PART III

*A*ll last night I tossed and turned, excitedly planning my life with Dennis, so when the telephone rings this morning shortly before eight o'clock, I feel like I've just gotten to sleep.

"It's Frank, Tess. Thought you'd be up and ready for Mass by now. You do know it's Sunday morning, don't you?"

"Of course I know it's Sunday, Frank," I retort groggily, irritably. "I just didn't expect it to come so early."

Frank ignores my crankiness and explains, "Wanted to catch you before you go to church because Rose is having a few people back afterwards and hoped you'd drop by. Got to milk every last vote you know."

I'm about to say that I'm intending to stay in bed and let God make house calls this morning because I'm still tired from milking votes at last night's bingo game, when Frank tells me that Dennis is to be the officiating priest at the service.

"The Holy Father will be saying the Mass." He says this as though it will be sufficient inducement for me to go, even if I am tired from vote garnering in the smoky bingo hall. "Father Ryan's mother or sister or some relative died and he had to leave in a hurry so he asked Dennis to fill in."

I begin to tremble violently, just as I did yesterday

afternoon when Dennis told me he was leaving the priesthood. My sensibilities simply cannot endure a picture of Dennis attired in liturgical vestments. An image of Mother's inert head on a cold pillow of pleated satin lances through my mind—an indelible image that for years had blocked out all benign images of her—and I know I must avoid housing a similar indelible image of an ecclesiastical Dennis. But even as I'm thinking these thoughts, my mind is already searching my closet for something suitable to wear and my body is checking its trembling and casting away its tiredness so it can send me off, to where my better judgement tells me I should not go.

I deliberately enter the church just late enough so there will be no chance of meeting Dennis in the vestibule. I choose a back pew, one that is behind a pillar, in the hope that I will be able to see him, but he won't be able to see me.

But even having taken these precautions, I'm not prepared for my reaction when Dennis walks out on the altar. Because it is a Sunday in Ordinary Times, he is wearing a green chasuble—green: the liturgical symbol of hope, worn after Epiphany and after Pentecost. Underneath the chasuble, he is wearing his alb and because it trails almost to the floor, I can only catch fleeting glimpses of his shoes as he walks across the altar. The white, long-sleeved linen alb symbolizes innocence and purity. Although I can't see it on account of the chasuble, I know a cord, symbolizing chastity and continence, cinches the flowing alb tight against Dennis' waist. The sleeves of the alb reach down to his wrist, and from elbow to wrist there is about a foot of fine lace.

I wonder whether Eileen made the lace. She was always crocheting or tatting and her furniture was covered with lace doilies. Pineapple doilies, Sarah would inform me. Whenever we were sent to the church after school to clean the wax from the candle holders on the altar and to scrape it off the floor in the sacristy, Sarah would point to the altar cloths and say, in a proud voice, "See that lace there? Mommy did that." She would toss her head imperially and tell us that her mother not only crocheted, she tatted as well. In fact, she tatted for Uncle Pat, the Jesuit. He had lace on all of his albs—tail and sleeves. I would become so viciously envious—the only laces my mother was associated with were the ones she put in the workboots on the assembly line—that I would jab at the hardened wax with the scraper until bits and pieces of candle flew off and stung my face.

I stare, as if transfixed, at Dennis' every movement and when he says, "In the name of the Father and of the Son and of the Holy Spirit," everyone but me makes the sign of the cross. I remain as if paralyzed. Then my eyes become fixated on Dennis' hands. I focus solely on his hands: those same hands that touched my hands, those same hands that touched my face, those same hands that touched my hair—touched me with such exquisite tenderness that even the sandpipers were jealous—are now touching the Sacred Vessels.

But, then, I can no longer see Dennis' hands because his mother's likeness rudely intrudes into my line of vision. Eileen is wearing her sealskin coat and sealskin hat, even though it is June and a very warm day. I fleetingly wonder whether she was buried in the sealskin coat. She had so liked to flaunt it because it had always set her apart from others in the Cove—from those who could only afford cloth coats. Eileen is sitting ramrod straight in her pew—a front pew, as befits the mother of an officiating priest. As I watch, she slowly turns from the altar to face me and impales me with accusing eyes. Shamed eyes. Joyless eyes. The eyes of the mother of a defrocked priest. And, then, most terrible of all, mirrored in this yawning anguish of Eileen's eyes are Dennis' eyes, regret chiselled into them so deeply that even he doesn't know it's there.

All strength leaves my body and I slump in the pew and grasp the padded seat for support. And suddenly everything becomes crystal clear, so clear that it seems as if I have been looking, as Paul wrote in his letters to the Corinthians, through a glass darkly. I see not only the present, I see the future. And it is a future filled with unspoken pain and excruciating, silent remorse. I wait for my chance and in the commotion of the congregation going to Communion I leave the church, forcing myself to tiptoe down the aisle, although I want to race down it and out to the parking lot where I will be able to get in my car and scream out my torment.

But once in the car, instead of screaming, I sit crouched over the steering wheel and whimper, dry-eyed. I whimper uselessly as I manoeuvre my way out of the parking lot and begin driving aimlessly around the Cove. I don't want to go home. I don't want to go to Rose's luncheon. I want only to see Dennis. I want to see him so I can convince him not to leave the priesthood. I must stop him before he goes to St. John's to talk to his friend.

But I can't determine how I will be able to get in touch with him. I dare not call his house in case Dolph or Sarah answers. At all costs, I don't want to arouse suspicion.

I drive around and around the Cove. I see people leaving the church and returning home after the service. I ask myself what excuse I can give to Frank if I don't turn up at Rose's luncheon and I know I can't manufacture one. And then, after several more trips up and down the road, I finally convince myself that I must phone Dennis, no matter what the risk.

I immediately compose an excuse to offer if Sarah answers the telephone. And one to offer if Dolph answers. I toss both of them away and compose better ones, and then toss these away as well. And I pull words together should luck be with me and Dennis answers. But for Dennis, whose love has completed me, my own words are pitifully inadequate, and I quickly cast them aside and muster together different ones—ones that aren't mine. *For everything there is a season. A time to weep and a time to laugh ... A time to gather stones and a time to scatter stones. A time to love ...*

I decide to wait until the confusion of the noon hour meal is over before I make the call. I go to Rose's luncheon, deciding it is easier to do so than to think up excuses for staying away. Distractedly, I wander around her living room, giving the right smiles and the right answers in the right places. I even show delight when I'm introduced as the Cove's next MHA. And I eat Rose's molded jellied salad without even tasting it. My mind is totally focused on the phone call that still isn't made. I leave just as soon as it is politely acceptable to do so.

My hands are so wet from perspiration that the telephone almost slips to the floor when I begin dialling Dolph's number.

"Hello."

It is Bernard's voice. Dolph's oldest boy. I'm so taken aback, I forget my rehearsed lines. Besides, I hadn't made any special lines in case the children answered.

"I'd like to speak to Dennis ... er, I mean Fr. Dennis."

"He's not here, Ma'am."

Disappointment drops to the bottom of my stomach like a rock to the bottom of a well. I have used up all my nerve in making this call, and to no avail. I can't leave a message, especially one requesting that Dennis call me.

"When do you expect him back?"

"Not till tomorrow night, Ma'am. He's gone to the funeral. Father Ryan's mother died."

"Are you certain he won't be back.?"

"That's what he said, Ma'am. That's all I know."

After I hang up the phone and have a few minutes to assess the situation, I convince myself that the call wasn't totally in vain. At least I got comforting information. If Dennis is with Father Ryan, he will not be able to go to St. John's in the morning, and with the election on Tuesday, he won't be able to leave the Cove then either. And if the election goes the way it is expected to go, I'll be able to see him at Dolph's headquarters when I go there to offer the customary best wishes from the vanquished to the victor. I'm certain that in the commotion and confusion of that evening, we'll be able to talk without attracting attention.

Now that I have found the time and place to tell Dennis what has to be told, all that is left for me to do is find the words for the telling. And the courage for the telling. I go upstairs to my bedroom to lie down, the phones muffled with cushions and pillows in case someone calls. I'm hoping wise words and stalwart courage will come to me as I huddle shrouded in Grandmother's quilts. And I'm hoping sleep will douse the climbing pain and accumulating emptiness that began making inroads into my soul the instant I saw Dennis' regret-filled eyes mirrored in the anguished ones of his mother. I'm also hoping that when I wake up it will be Wednesday:

the election will be over, I will have told Dennis, and I will be heading back to St. John's and to my job at the travel agency.

Somewhere deep down inside me, where denial clings, I have never thought that election day would actually arrive. But if I had any doubts this morning, Frank's early call to say this is *It*, sharply italicizing the word, was certainly enough to bring me to reality. Indeed, on account of *It*, the headquarters has been in total turmoil all day long and now that the polls have closed and we are awaiting the returns, excitement is at full peak.

This morning, Greg and Frank rearranged the kitchen, clearing out the couch side of the room so that Greg could plaster the wall with plain brown paper. He drew columns down the paper, one column for each Party. There are fifteen polls in all and he has allocated a space for each poll. He has also written in the returns from the last election so he can do an on-the-spot analysis of where gains and losses are made.

Right now, every inch of floor space is occupied with people. The noise is deafening. So far two polls have been heard from. To everyone's amazement, I have won one poll by a slight margin and I am trailing Dolph by only a few votes in the second one. No one expected this much success for me, so now, even I, decked out in my Liberal-red cotton skirt and blouse, am getting caught up in the excitement.

While Greg keeps the score, Frank answers the phone and sometimes he has to shout at the crowd, to silence them long enough for him to hear the returns. For the past several minutes the phone hasn't rung and the noise level has increased with each uninterrupted minute. Snippets of conversations fall here and there like confetti in the wind. One man is complaining to a cluster of people that his wife is spending his money faster than he can bring it in.

"I keeps telling her we'll be back on the cursed dole if she don't let up," he says, clutching a glass of beer close to his vest so it won't get jostled. "I swear to God every beggar and pedlar that comes across the Gulf asks their way to Gladys' house, knowing she'll pony up with my money." He stops, takes a mouthful of beer and continues. "And I don't mind the beggars so much. I remembers the time I needed a handout. I was up in Botwood. Went up to look for work in the lumberwoods and got stranded and this Salvation Army fellow came along and took the coat off his back and gave it to me. And took me to his place for a bowl of soup. I'll never forget it as long as I live."

The telephone rings and Frank grabs the receiver. Cupping his hand over the mouthpiece, he shouts across the room.

"Shut up! The bunch of you! This place is like a bloody lunatic asylum. Couldn't hear Judgement Day, much less the returns."

Bit by bit, talk peters out until there is just a low hum.

Frank turns back to the phone and hollers into it, "What was that? What did ye say?" His tone takes a sudden drop. "Oh my Christ! Oh no! Oh my Christ!"

The room silences instantly and we all stare at him. He slowly puts the phone back in its cradle and lowers himself into his chair. "Dolph's headquarters. That's who that was," he says after a few seconds, shaking his head as if he has just awakened from a nightmare and wants to jolt himself awake. "There's been an accident. A God-awful one. Dolph and young Dennis Walsh. The priest." There is a sound in the room as if everyone in unison has hauled in their breath, waiting. Someone whispers in a desperate childish voice, "Oh please God. No! Oh please God, No!" and I realize the words are coming from my mouth.

Frank pulls out a handkerchief and mops his face and then elaborates. "They were driving to the polls and a car from St. John's. Bird hunters going on the Shore ... Drunk as skunks ... Dolph escaped without a scratch, but Dennis ... well Dennis ... Dennis was ... Well my Christ Almighty, Dennis is in bad shape. Real bad shape."

I try to scream and the air rushes out of my lungs so that all I can do is stand crushed up against the kitchen table, mutely opening and closing my mouth like a fish drowning in air. I once had a propane stove explode in an apartment I was renting and the air was sucked out of the room in one gigantic swoosh and I had to take short, gulping breaths to keep from fainting. This same heavy blackness swirls around me now, but I can't find the strength to breathe. I grope behind my back to get a grip on the table and feel myself sliding to the floor. Greg is suddenly beside me, breaking my fall. He buoys me upright and manoeuvres me through the crowd and into the parlour. Behind me I hear the kitchen begin to fill up with talk again, but this time with a difference. The talk is hushed, whispered, like in church before the service starts. Greg leads me to the velvet chair and I huddle into it while he goes to get me a glass of water. As soon as he leaves, voices from yesterday visit me once more, but this time they come to comfort, not to chastise. They are gentle and low and as soft as the darkness.

"Poor Little Rabbit. Gram will make ye buttermilk biscuits. And Martin will play ye a tune. Won't ye Martin? Go on, boy, tell her ye will."

"Sure I will, girl. I'll play yer favourite. *She's Like a Swallow*. But you got to stop yer blubberin'. See! I've got the mouth organ in my pocket. But, remember, you got to sing the words. I'm not goin' to play if you won't sing along." He coaxes, "Come on now! Let's start." The parlour fills with music. Sad music. *She's like a swallow that flies on high. She's like a river that never runs dry.* He stops playing, and although I can't see him, I know he is rubbing the harmonica across his pant leg to wipe it dry. He again coaxes, but this time his patience is straining. "All right then, if you won't sing that one, let's try *Isle of Capri*. That's your next favourite." He begins playing. *On the Isle of Capri I did meet her. In the shade of the old walnut tree.*

Greg eases open the parlour door and in the dark creeps to my chair. He squats down beside me and gives me the water.

"I'm very sorry, Tess," he says, compassionately, not letting go of the glass in case my ice cold hands will drop it. "I know how hard it is. I had a special friend once. She died of leukemia."

Frank's voice cuts short our conversation. "What's going on Tess? I saw you leave." His eyes adjust to the darkness and he sees my huddled form. "Holy God, don't cave in on us now, girl. The returns are coming in fast and furious. And you're neck and neck with Dolph. And the only way to count the people out there now would be to turn them out in the meadow. Thicker than a school of spawning capelin."

When I neither move, nor speak, he softens his words. "I know you were good friends with Dennis, girl, and 'tis shockin' about what happened. But we're hopin' he'll be alright. And Dolph's headquarters just called back and said they took him to St. Clare's. And you know they can do wonders in there. Practically rebuild someone." He says, more to Greg than to me, so that Greg will know we won't be making the trek over to Dolph's headquarters. "Dolph went to St. John's with him. In the hearse. Won't be back out tonight."

"Fine, Frank!" Greg responds. "You keep things

going out there. Get Bill to mark up the returns. Tess just needs a little time." He reaches for a handkerchief in his breast coat pocket and passes it to me. "As soon as she gets her bearings, we'll be back out. Just say the heat got to her."

"We did it! By God, we did it! A squeaker, but a miss is as good as a mile," Frank hollers out the instant he gets the results from the final poll. A raucous shout immediately goes up in the headquarters and two men grab me and hold me aloft on their shoulders. Everyone begins singing "For She's a Jolly Good Fellow" as I'm paraded around the kitchen, the porch and the dining room. They even take me out in the yard where people are hanging around waiting for space to open up so they can get inside. I wave and shake hands and pretend to be as exhiliarated as everyone else, but my heart is empty and my victory is hollow. My one thought is to get to Greg to ask him to call Dolph's headquarters again to see if there is any news.

"Speech! Speech!" someone shouts. Right away the chant is picked up by the crowd. "Speech! Speech! Speech!"

I realize, in panic, I don't have anything prepared for a victory speech. Greg and I had talked over the things I should say in my vanquished speech at Dolph's headquarters, but all along the possibility of winning had seemed so remote that nothing had been prepared in case of victory. And, of course, this evening, on account of Dennis' accident, the furthest thing from my mind has been speechmaking. I hastily muster together befitting thoughts, my mind running through a list of people whose names I must remember in order to acknowledge their help.

"Speech! Speech! Speech!"

Frank, assuming I have my speech well under control, announces that everyone should go outside— that I'll be speaking in a few minutes in the front yard. He gets a chair and brings it outside and positions it in the middle of the quickly reassembling crowd. I'm carried out on the shoulders of the two men who have been parading me around the headquarters. I climb upon the chair as Frank is testing it for balance, and all the while I'm moving about I'm hastily pulling together what I must say. I take several big breaths and then begin.

"Ladies and Gentlemen, Fellow Liberals: this is a grand night for you. This is a grand night for me. And this is a grand night for the Liberal Party in the Cove." There is deafening applause and I wait for it to die down before continuing. "With your help, we have made history here tonight—the first Liberal win for the Cove and the first woman MHA for Newfoundland." Again, there is wild applause. I mention the committee members whose names I must single out individually. I thank the members of the Women's Liberal Association. I thank the poll workers. I thank the people who permitted signs to be placed on their premises. I thank the people who volunteered to drive voters to the polls. I reserve my final and special thanks for Greg and Frank. I reaffirm my commitment to the Party and to the issues that formed my platform. I congratulate my opponent on his good showing at the polls. And then, because it must be done, I bolster my courage to mention the accident. I say that our joy in victory is diminished by the news of Father Dennis Walsh's terrible accident, and that on behalf of the Cove Liberals, we offer our sympathy to the Simmons family and our prayers for the speedy recovery of Father Dennis.

The mention of the accident causes the applause

to be more muted than it would have been otherwise and soon people are moving about, talking to each other and eating the sandwiches that the Liberal Women's Association has brought in. I accept individual congratulations as I walk across the room to where Greg is leaning against the wall.

"Well done!" he says, putting a comradely arm around my shoulder. Then, anticipating my question, he updates me on the accident. "No more news. Just that he's still in the operating room."

Frank pushes his way through the crowd and joins us.

"Great stuff!" he exults, his face flushed from the heat and from the victory. "Stick-handled yer way through that speech with no trouble atall. Thanked the ones that should be thanked. And speaking ..." He pauses as if wondering whether there will be a better time to say what he has to say, and then decides this is as good a time as any. He continues, "And speaking of thanking, I want you never to forget them that put you there."

I'm quite taken aback. Although Frank always speaks his mind, he has never been one to try and curry favour. When I gather my composure, I ask, "Are you saying you want a job in government, Frank?" To lessen his embarrassment, especially since Greg has been listening, I joke, "God help you if you have to depend on my meager influence to get into government."

He flusters, "Naw! Naw! Not fer meself. You couldn't pry me away from the Cove with a crowbar." He shakes his head in Rose's direction. "And besides I wouldn't want you living that close to her. Put too many notions in her head. Already told me she's going to resign from the Women's Liberal Association to get involved in ..." He pauses momentarily, searching for the correct articulation of such a hoity-toity aspiration, "the mainstream association. Says the boys can make their own sandwiches." He looks at Greg and guffaws. "Be God, the next thing ye knows, I'll be peelin' the potatoes and makin' the beds."

Someone comes by and asks Greg a question about removing the posters and when his attention is diverted, Frank jerks his thumb towards Greg and says, "He's what I was talking about. Don't ferget him."

When Greg rejoins our conversation, I say lightly, "Frank is admonishing me not to forget you when I come into my kingdom. Says when I get to be Premier, I should make you my Solicitor General."

Greg is obviously discomfitted by the turn of the conversation, but he rejoins in a bantering manner, "*Solicitor General*! No way! I'm not going to call in my tokens until you get to be Prime Minister. I'm angling for Governor General. Or a seat on the Senate."

"I'll buy that," I reply quickly and then hesitate only a second before adding mischievously, "I'll ask Rose to be Solicitor General."

Frank waves his hands as if Greg and I are beyond redemption and then he moves off to rejoin the crowd. Greg and I look at each other and both of us laugh, I for the first time since I heard about Dennis' accident.

This morning, the morning after the election, Dolph arrives at my house as I am in the midst of cleaning up overflowing ashtrays and slopped-over styrofoam cups. He looks haggard. I know he has come to do the polite thing—to offer congratulations from vanquished to victor—and I know this mission isn't easy for him. To place us on easier ground, I immediately ask about Dennis, hoping Dolph has more up-to-date information than what I have received this morning from Greg.

Dolph lets out his breath heavily and sits down in a chair by the door. I pull up a chair beside him.

"Dennis is not good," he says. "Not good at all. The head injuries have been looked after, but we're not sure about internal injuries yet."

He fidgets. "But I didn't come just to talk about Dennis." He puts a cigarette in his mouth and fumbles with his cigarette lighter, but because his hands are trembling it takes him a few seconds to ignite it. After a few strokes of his thumb on the ignition wheel, the flame spurts out and he lights his cigarette, then takes a long drag and slowly expels the smoke.

He says, "I came by to offer you congratulations. You surprised a lot of people. Me included."

Because I don't want to be perceived as gloating, I say, "Well it's me today. Someone else tomorrow. That's the way politics goes."

"That's for sure," he agrees, looking relieved that he now has the worst part of his mission over with. "And it's only when something like this happens, like this accident, that you get things in the right place. You see what's important and what's not."

He ponders a moment, takes another long drag on the cigarette and again slowly exhales the smoke.

"Tess," he says, squinting at me through the smoke, "I came for a second reason." He rushes his words as if to get it all out in the open in a hurry. "I came for Dennis. He asked to see you. And I wouldn't wait around if I were you. I'd go in today. Sarah is coming out this morning for a change of clothing. So this afternoon would be a good time. You won't cross paths."

I ask myself if I can be hearing correctly. *Dennis asked Dolph to get in touch with me and Dolph is clearing the way so I won't have to contend with Sarah?* Dolph sees the shock that is registering on my face and he quickly explains. "Oh I've known about you two. I saw you on the beach together one afternoon when I went for a drive. And I guessed the rest. And last night when we were driving around, going from poll to poll ... well ... we talked. Dennis was saying he couldn't understand why receiving one Sacrament should prevent him from receiving another. You know, Holy Orders and Matrimony. And I figured it had to do with you, although I never said as much to him."

I'm so completely flabbergasted, my breath is almost taken away. I manage to ask, "Are you telling me you *knew* Dennis and I were meeting and you never said anything to anyone? You kept *that* to yourself?" I'm so taken off guard, I begin to stammer. "But ... but ... you could have ... you had it in your power to destroy me. One breath of that before the election, even though it was innocent enough ... well you could have done me damage."

He looks around for an ashtray, and seeing they are all overflowing, he settles for dropping the ash in his cupped fist. I'm so stupified by what has just been said that I make no effort to get up and dump the ashtrays so he can have an empty one. He pays no notice, but continues to use his hand.

"If I'd have said anything, I would've hurt Sarah in the bargain. She idolizes Dennis. And like I told you when I saw you at Bowerings, Sarah and the children mean more to me than any election."

I feel compelled to defend my association with Dennis. "Dolph, Dennis and I were never more than friends. We go back such a long way together. And I would never do anything to hurt him."

"Well, I hope you wouldn't, Tess," Dolph says, in a tone that is more matter-of-fact than threatening. "And Dennis wouldn't hurt you either. He told me as much. But whatever you may think, Dennis was born for the priesthood, Tess." Between puffs of smoke he adds, "He wouldn't be contented for long outside it."

Dolph then explains that only family members can get in to see Dennis, and only for a few minutes at a time, but he has put my name on the list of family. "Just give them your name at the desk. I arranged everything."

"I'll leave right now," I say, wishing I were already on the road. "I'd rather be waiting in there than out here."

Having said what he came to say, Dolph gets up to go. This time I have the presence of mind to get him an ashtray so he can empty his fist before going outside. As I'm thanking Dolph for bringing me word of Dennis, I recall that when Frank first talked to me about Dolph, he described him as mamby-pamby. I didn't exactly know what he meant by the term, but I knew it had something to do with lack of emotional strength. I am now sure that Frank miscalled that one.

<p>

Dennis is impaled to his bed by needles and tubes. His head is swathed in bandages. His face is as white as the pillowcases. His eyes are closed, and because the nurse told me he is sleeping, I tiptoe to the side of his bed. His eyes flutter open the minute I come near.

"Tessie, you came!" His voice is weak, but his delight in my presence is apparent in every word.

The rail protectors are up on the bed, preventing me from sitting on it, so I lean over him, very close so he won't have to strain. He tries to move his hand to touch me. "No. No. Don't move. Don't move," I say quickly, reaching over and gently brushing his fingers with mine. "Please don't move. You might disturb the needles."

I ache to touch his face, to kiss his lips, but because the nurse is constantly present, fiddling with monitors and tubes, I have to refrain from doing anything that a concerned relative wouldn't do.

"Congratulations, Tessie," Dennis says, so soft-voiced I can hardly hear him. "Dolph told me."

For the first time since my win at the polls last night, it dawns on me what this victory of mine must mean to Dennis. In the surprise of the win and in the confusion of his accident, it only occurs to me now that the win for me means a loss for him.

I'm so anguished by this thought that when I speak, my voice is almost as weak as Dennis'. "I'm so sorry, Dennis. I'm so very, very sorry. Please forgive me." I reach out and touch his hand again and lightly brush my fingers over his. "I had no idea I was going to win. You know that. No idea in the world. When you get better, we'll talk. But for now just get well."

He focuses his eyes on mine, holding the stare so that, even though I know the nurse may be watching, I cannot look away.

"Many waters cannot quench love. Neither can the floods drown it," he says, whispering so faintly that if I didn't know the quotation from the *Song of Solomon*, I wouldn't be able to distinguish what he is saying.

My eyes fill to the brim with tears and rivulets of water shamelessly rain down my face. All of my resolve to be circumspect disappears and I stoop down and brush my lips against his, letting them linger there for only the briefest of moments.

When I pull away, he gives me a wan smile and closes his eyes again. I look at him lying there so still and I recall his vitality during those days at the beach; his strong sun-tanned arms; his hearty laugh. I pray that this vitality will see him through now.

The nurse comes over to tell me that my visiting time is up. As I get up to leave, I impulsively stoop down and once more touch Dennis' lips with my own.

"I'll be back," I say, very, very softly, just in case he is sleeping.

But he lets me know he is still awake, by whispering, "Be happy, my Tessie. At last you have your centre."

After I've gathered myself together I decide that, while I'm in St. John's, I should stop at the travel agency to make a phone call to the head office. Soon after my win I made up my mind that if I am fortunate enough to be given a portfolio, I will devote my full time to it. In this case it will be necessary for me to make arrangements with Sperry to have someone take over my job. I call the Montreal office and acquaint them with the situation. I make a quick trip to my apartment to check with my landlord and then I begin the drive back home.

Along the way my mind goes back to the centre Dennis spoke about—the one I had always searched for; the one that had always eluded me. I tell myself that one of these days, when he comes back from Peru, I'll be able to show him that college in the Cove. And I'll show him the new wing, outfitted like an infirmary, on the old age home. Perhaps even a spanking new ambulance will be parked beside the hearse.

I also tell myself that, by then, maybe time will have eased the heartache for both of us, although it seems so very unlikely at this moment. I'm wishing I could rush the months forward.

Dennis is dead. Frank called this morning. "Tess," he

said, and I had never before heard such compassion in his voice, "Did you hear?"

"Did I hear what?" I asked.

"About poor Dennis. My God Almighty, girl, he died. Last night. His lungs filled up."

The kitchen walls swam around me in ever-widening circles and I was catapulted back into Dennis' hospital room. I could hear again his last gentle words to me: *Be happy, my Tessie.* Now I was certain that he knew he was going to die, no matter what the prognosis for his recovery was.

Frank sensed my absence and asked, "Tess! Are you there? Where did you go?"

"I haven't gone anywhere Frank," I lied. "I just had to pull the kettle off the front burner."

Frank spun out details. "He went just before midnight. Dolph said he seemed to be alright yesterday evening when he was in. And, of course, you were there in the afternoon and he was alright then?"

This last was a question, and I answered it simply. "Yes," I said. "He was alright when I saw him."

Frank then told me he was going to send Rose up to explain everything to me. "She's on her way right now. She's a trained nurse, you remember. And she said this sort of thing often happens. Pneumonia sets in and 'tis not the injury that takes the person, but the pneumonia."

Although I wanted to be alone right then more than anything else in the world, I didn't have the energy to argue with Frank. So I sat on the couch and waited for Rose to come to my house. But I knew her trip would be in vain. How much explaining would it take to make me understand why Dennis had been snatched so prematurely from the world?

The soft light in the funeral parlour erases the strain from Sarah's eyes. Once again I can see my childhood sparring partner, the young girl who always knew who she was—niece of Jesuit priest, cousin of Franciscan nun. She is standing in the centre of the room, talking to the funeral director who is jotting down instructions for the funeral.

As soon as I go to her, and before I have a chance to offer condolences, she surprises me by pulling me into the conversation.

"I'm right, aren't I Tess?" Her eyes sweep from me to the funeral director, drawing the three of us together. "Laity are brought into the church feet first, but priests go in head first." She punctuates the truth of her statement by calling in Sr. Clarence as an authority. "That's what Sr. Clarence always said. Remember when we took liturgical studies?"

It is the sort of information Sarah would be likely to remember after almost fifteen years, and the sort that I would be likely to forget almost immediately. However, since I have seldom been called upon to put forth a noble lie on Sarah's behalf, and because Dennis is hammered shut inside the burnished mahogany casket at the other side of the room, his body too injured to be publicly displayed in priestly garb, I lie easily, "Yes, that's right, Sarah. I remember Sr. Clarence saying that very thing many times. It's symbolic of something or other. I forget what."

Sarah gives the funeral director one of her imperial looks, so reminiscent of her mother's—a look that says her priest-brother will get the special recognition that he deserves and he will not be rolled up the aisle toes first like the rest of the Cove folk. As I make my way over to Dennis, I wonder what he would have to say about such nonsense and I think that all Sarah needs to become the reincarnation of Eileen is a sealskin coat.

Dennis was buried today. I went to the funeral mass, but not to the cemetery. I didn't want to see him being lowered into the ground, although I did enquire from Frank the location of his grave. He told me it was only a few feet below the brow of the hill and just a spit in the wind from the Corrigan family plot.

I drove to the beach as soon as the mass was over. I took off my sandals when I got out of the car and walked barefoot over the warm, smooth rocks. The wind was gentle and it wrapped my silky skirt close to my body, caressing my thighs and my calves. The sun shone on my face, stroking my skin. I walked along until I came to the large boulder that formed the windbreak for our sheltered place, and then I stopped and rummaged in my purse for a nail file and gouged Dennis' initials into the boulder's water-smooth face. I even added his clerical affiliation:

D.W. SFM, 1970

I chiselled with the determination of a Rodin or a Michelangelo, cutting trenches so deep it will take years for the sea to wear them level. And as I chiselled, I told Dennis that I didn't need his initials carved in stone for me to remember him. I said I would think of him always. I would think of him in the morning and in the evening, but particularly in the evening because even gentle memories become more gentle after the sun goes down.

Directly underneath his initials, I carved my own, and I added the letters to which I am now entitled by virtue of my victory at the polls.

T.C. MHA, 1970

On the walk back to the car, I hugged the landwash. The tide lopped lazily against the shore, each wave inching further and further up the beach as if to tantalize my feet. A pair of sandpipers strutted ahead of me, bobbing their way to a sandy shoal just abreast of the lighthouse. The soft, inland wind continued to nuzzle my skirt against my legs, and from somewhere high in the cliffs overlooking our sheltered place, a seagull screeched its rage.

M.T. (Jean) DOHANEY was born in Point Verde, a small coastal village on the Avalon Peninsula of Newfoundland. Her first novel, *The Corrigan Women*, (Ragweed Press, 1987) evoked the raw environment of Newfoundland life in its depiction of matriarchal survival and courage. Her second book, a collection of journal entries called *When Things Get Back to Normal* (Pottersfield Press) was also published to wide acclaim. She has a Masters of Education and a Doctorate of Education in English. She currently teaches technical writing at the University of New Brunswick in Fredericton.

THE BEST OF RAGWEED PRESS

℘ *The Corrigan Women,* **M.T. Dohaney** A poignant and humorous tale of three generations of Newfoundland women. Rural life draws grandmother, mother and daughter together, but the increasing influence of the outside world challenges them to evolve while maintaining loyalty to their environment and their true selves. ISBN 0-920304-67-2 $10.95

℘ *Dark Jewels,* **Rita Donovan** A haunting first novel set in Cape Breton, which explores three generations of a family in conflict, the economic poverty of the coal mines and the spiritual poverty tha' exists within a family. Donovan involves us in a richly imagined and desolate universe, depicting lives that demand our compassion and extend our humanity. ISBN 0-921556-04-7 $10.95

℘ *The Husband,* **Dorothy Livesay** Written in the late 1960s, this novella by one of the nation's best known poets, explores estrangement and reconciliation in marriage, through a series of letter from Celia, a forty-five-year-old painter in search of love and independence. ISBN 0-921556-02-0 $8.95

℘ *Lnu and Indians We're Called,* **Rita Joe** Micmac poet Rita Joe's third collection of poetry follows and expands upon her desire to communicate gently with her own people and to reach out to the wider community. She invites us to "Listen to me, the spiritua Indian." ISBN 0-921556-22-5 $9.95

℘ *The Miraculous Hand and Other Stories,* **J.J. Steinfeld** This highly original short story collection is informed by a Jewish sensibility and a singular vision of the grotesque—the gift of "genuine black humour" that is the trademark of Steinfeld's fiction.   ISBI 0-921556-15-2 $10.95

℘ *The New Poets of Prince Edward Island,* **Catherine Matthews (ed** Thirty Island poets writing from the period 1980 to 1990 treat us landscapes, portraits, confessions, witticisms and treatises that refle the physical, emotional and spiritual convolutions inherent i Island-dwelling. ISBN 0-921556-07-1 $14.95

℘ *She Tries Her Tongue: Her Silence Softly Breaks,* **Marlene Nourbes Philip** "A political statement of the coming to power of voice, ar the passion and persistence of black female resistance." (*Fuse*) Winn of the prestigious Casa de las Americas Prize in 1988. ISBN 0-921556-03-9 $9.95

RAGWEED PRESS books can be found in quality bookstores, or individu orders may be sent prepaid to: RAGWEED PRESS, P.O. Box 20: Charlottetown, Prince Edward Island, Canada, C1A 7N7. Please add posta and handling ($1.50 for the first book and 75 cents for each additional boc to your order. Canadian residents add 7% GST to the total amount. G registration no. R104383120.